I0776442

CIRCLE OF FREAKS

ALSO BY
DELILAH CROWW

WHISPERS IN THE DARK

CIRCLE OF FREAKS

DELILAH CROWW

Ivy Sloan

Since I was a little girl, I fell in love with the circus. It's all I ever wanted to see up close or be a part of. There was no room for things like that where I grew up. There was no room for anything except bad memories and bad expectations.

Every year around Devil's Night, since we moved to Stockbridge, the Circle of Freaks paranormal circus comes to town. It's an eighteen-and-over horror show in which no one talks about what goes on inside because they can't.

But this year is different. This year, my prayers have been answered by gifting me a ticket. Despite what people think of me at school. Despite the girls gone missing— Found dead. I wasn't prepared for what I would see. I wasn't prepared for…him.

I could die a million times, and our love would always bring me back to you.

DRACO

There is one and the same soul in many bodies.
    Plotinus

CHAPTER ONE

I STARE at the wall with all the scuffs of dirt that needed paint. The kind you wonder how they got there or if the wall is even worth painting over because it will look the same a few weeks later. I wonder how much longer. How much longer will it be before I get out of this shithole.

When you have money, that wouldn't matter. You would paint it. Except for those who earn a paycheck above poverty—for people like us, that isn't an option. And if you live at the Meadow River apartment complex in Stockbridge, Massachusetts. The ones who couldn't pay their light and rent in the same month.

The Meadow River apartment building is old. It still has the box air conditioners that hung out the windows. Some have duct tape to make sure it wouldn't fall out.

According to state law, a landlord is not required to provide air-conditioning. When the summer heat came, I had to walk around half naked. We didn't have enough for the electric bill. Like most tenants living in Meadow River, they had to choose the rent or the air conditioner in the summer.

I pour the last few drops of milk into my cereal bowl. A sheen of sweat coats my forehead. I look at the dry cereal, debating whether to throw it out or eat it dry. I walk over to the sink and turn on the faucet, adding some water into the bowl. Placing it down, I check the time. Ten minutes before the bus pulls out front.

I mix the cereal with water and milk with my spoon, close my eyes, and take a bite. It's not the worst I've tasted, but it sucks to eat cereal with water.

I take a deep breath, checking the time again, bracing myself for my last year of high school. Three minutes.

If it were up to my mother, she would have told me to hell with it and ask for my hours back at the grocery store. I repeated the eleventh grade because I had so many absences and failed all my classes. I had no choice but to skip school that year and get a job or risk getting evicted. My mother doesn't make enough at the diner she works at, so it's up to me to help with rent.

The kitchen light goes out. I drop my spoon with a clank and open the front door to see if the yellow light in the hallway is still on. If we were a couple of days late paying the electric bill, the first thing I did was look outside to see if anyone else's light was still on. If it's not, it's a blackout. If it is, our light was shut off for non-payment.

Looking up, I let out a relieved breath. It's a blackout. I have to ask my mother if she paid the bill before the shut-off date. If not, we wait until I get paid from work or when my side hustle comes through.

Grabbing my bag and dropping the bowl in the sink, I head out, locking the door behind me. The Meadow apartments aren't bad compared to where I lived my freshman year in South Carolina. This place beats the trailer park filled with meth addicts. This was the best my mother could do, coming from a background of jobless addicts and prostitutes.

I walk down the stairs because the elevators are out of order, which is no surprise. They smell like piss anyway.

The obscene graffiti was something that always stood out. It was on the neighbor's doors and the walls in the hallway in big black letters sprayed over the peeling paint. Some were on the elevator doors. No one complained that the building hadn't been painted. It looks like it's been that way since the early seventies. No one wanted the place to look too nice for fear they would raise the rent, and we would all get screwed.

I look at the thoughtful message, SUCK COCK. It has a picture of two big testicles with a gigantic penis drawn above it and, SMOKE AND FUCK. The messages changed every so often. No one knew who did it, and the security guard was too busy sleeping on the night shift to give a shit about it. There were no cameras or daytime security. Anyone could come inside the building, which was disconcerting.

The yellow public school bus arrives on cue with FUCK SCHOOL spray painted on the side. The apartment complex is behind the Stockbridge Mall. The drive-in theater behind the mall is called the Coyote Drive-In. The drive-in plays one new release and three classic movies every week.

Stockbridge was founded in the seventeen hundreds.A forest surrounds the whole town. It has old architecture and historic homes on the west side of the school. A fair also opens when it is above thirty-eight degrees in the colder months. Stockbridge High is the middle ground. The center of it all. Where the teenagers meet, graduate, and go their separate ways.

I hop on the bus, ignoring the smirks and stares aimed my way. The bus gets on the highway from the parking lot that separates the plaza from the apartment complex. The only way to reach this side of Stockbridge is the main highway. It's old, and no one comes to this side unless you live here or want to park to watch a movie or the mall. No one goes to the plaza. Everyone knows that is the last thing people do at drive-ins. It's an excuse to park your car with dark-tinted windows so you can fuck in the back seat.

I should know. It's how I lost my virginity my sopho-more year in the back seat of the star quarterback's Mustang. He said the right things to get me to go out with him.

It didn't even hurt the first time, and every time I think about it, I hate myself for being so stupid. I didn't care about losing my virginity. I had to lose it to someone, but I should have done it with someone else. Not a six-foot-two, tanned skin, ash-blond hair, blue-eyed asshole like Tommy Hill.

After reading about how perfect and magical sex and love were supposed to be, I realized how bad at sex he was. A girl like me didn't expect love. Not where I came from or how I was raised. When we moved to Stock-bridge, I wanted to fit in. I wanted to experience what I read about, and no one knew where I came from. I thought Tommy was different, and he knew what he was doing since he was so good on the football field. I wasn't prepared for how bad it would be.

I can feel Tommy's hot breath on my neck. He rubs his fingers over my clit to get me wet. His fingers are rough and uncoordinated. I watched enough porn on my piece of shit cell phone in my bedroom to see how it was done. He shoves into me, and I expect a burn from him penetrating my barrier, but nothing—a lot of rubbing and no sparks.

He looks up, and I make the same face I saw the girl getting fucked on my phone. It works. He ate it up.

"Oh fuck. Ivy. You feel so good and tight, baby. Oh…fuck."

But it was over before it began. I could feel nothing, but he couldn't tell by the fake noises I made.

He grips my legs on the uncomfortable back seat of his Mustang and trembles like he has the chills.

When he's done, he lies on top of me, out of breath, the seat belt buckle digging into my lower back. I feel hot and sweaty. I wince when he goes soft, sliding out of me like a tampon.

"You were amazing. Did it feel good, Ivy?"

I paste a fake smile when he looks up. "You were perfect."

I want to cry. I hate it. He plants a wet kiss on my mouth, finally getting off me.

The next day at school, I found out we were both liars, but for very different reasons.

CHAPTER TWO

WALKING through the doors of Stockbridge High on the first day of school, I ignore the stares. Most of the popular guys at Stockbridge are jocks hoping to get into a D1 school to escape their parents. Girls from rich families have nothing to worry about when they graduate. The rest of them are rich kids who smoke weed and snort coke and live for the weekend. Like every school, there are the students who get picked on for fun because they are broke or didn't fit in popular society.

Every school had a group of kids like that. The nerd or the emo kid who didn't wear the right clothes and wasn't good enough to get the attention.

The halls echo with people walking, door lockers slamming open and closed. Guys lean against the wall making out, while feeling up their girlfriends.

I make it to my locker, ignoring Jason smirking at me with his shoulder against the wall. My eyes roll when I see what they wrote over my locker in huge black letters when I spin the dial.

IVY SLOAN IS A SLUT

Five guys from the football team show up next to Jason, including Tommy.

"Hey, Ivy," Jason mocks. He clears his throat like he's getting ready for a speech. "I had a hard-on this morning. You should have seen it. I thought of three letters and remembered your name when I had my hand around my dick."

I grab the two textbooks I need for my next two classes, slam the locker closed, and turn my head. "I guess there wasn't much to grab, being that my name has only three letters."

"Damn, Jason. You got a small dick," one of them says, laughing behind me as I walk away.

"That is exactly what a slut would say!" Jason yells over the noise in the hallway.

Walking into my US history class, I take a seat in the back. After a few minutes, a girl with straight black hair walks in. Her name is Alice. I heard she grew up here in Stockbridge and lives in an old estate on the west side.

"Watch it, Freak," the guy blocking the aisle says when Alice tries to step over his shoes.

She sits beside me, and I give her a tight-lipped smile. She looks like she hasn't slept. The dark circles under her eyes don't hide how gorgeous she is. I wonder why they call her a freak, but she must wonder why they call me a slut.

School drones on. When it's the end of the day and I open my locker, a flyer slides out. The flyer has a black-and-white circus tent with red letters on the top that read,

CIRCLE OF FREAKS PARANORMAL CIRCUS OF

HORROR IS COMING BACK TO STOCKBRIDGE.
COME IF YOU DARE. 18 AND OVER TO PLAY.

I smile to myself because I tried to go last year when I turned eighteen but didn't have the money. A paranormal circus fascinates me, but you had to be an adult to go. I heard they travel to warmer states when it gets cold up north. The bottom of the flyer reads in fine print that the show is for adults only. You have to sign a waiver, and you cannot bring your phones inside the show.

The fair in town is from August through November. Two sides mirror each other at the entrance. One side is a traditional fair with carnival rides and games. The other is the Carnevil of Horror filled with haunted houses and themed for Halloween. A side entrance is for adults only, where the Circle of Freaks paranormal circus is set up. I've never been to either fair, but I've seen pictures online.

I pocket the flyer, hoping I could go this year, wondering how I will come up with the money. I scoured the internet to see if I could find anything on YouTube to see what goes on inside the tent, but I came up empty.

A blaring sound goes off, echoing through the hallway. I look at my phone and notice an amber alert for another missing girl. That's the fifth one this year. The Stockbridge police assumed the first incident was a runaway teenager. That was until they found her body beaten and raped. Then the second, third, and fourth girls went missing.

After a couple of months, they found their bodies. They were all tortured and raped and found in different parts of the state. The first one was Mandy Walsh. They found her body floating in a lake five miles from the edge of town. The second was Emily Bowden. They found her body near the tree line in a black garbage bag near the main highway. It made headlines across the news channels. More girls came up missing in different states, all found in the same condition. Some are still missing from other states. Experts say that it's part of a human trafficking ring targeting teenage girls. They've warned everyone to stay vigilant and for parents to talk to their kids about reporting someone suspicious and not walk home alone. But some of us don't have a choice.

The bus lets me off at the stop near the Big H grocery mart. It is the only grocery store in town and the only place hiring my junior year. Kevin, the manager, is a middle-aged asshole who hates his wife and works open to close to avoid having to go home.

The parking lot is not as full in the afternoon on Mondays as I make my way across it. A plumbing store called Down to Flush is next to the grocery store. The employees wear shirts with DTF written in big gold letters on the back. When I first saw an employee with the shirt, I couldn't get over the owner using DTF as its logo. DTF to us teenagers means Down To Fuck. It hasn't hindered their business when they go out to service their customers.

I walk inside and head to the employee locker room to change out of my school uniform.

"Hey, Ivy." Kevin greets me with a smile. His eyes linger on the hem of my skirt where it ends mid-thigh.

"Hi Kevin, how's the wife?"

His eyes scroll up my thighs, licking his lips, making me cringe. Kevin has a belly that hangs slightly over his belt. I wonder if he can still see his dick. He's balding and has beady eyes, but in his mind, he thinks he's good-looking.

"She's…home," he answers finally when his eyes land on my face.

"Say hi to her for me."

His eyes harden because we both know he will do no such thing. I'm also not stupid enough to believe that I got this job for any other reason than for his personal sick fantasy. But beggars can't be choosers, and as much as I want to tell him to stick the cashier position up his ass, I can't.

After changing into the cashier uniform, which is a white dress shirt Kevin ordered a size too small, I try to pull the vest to hide my cleavage the best I can and fix my name tag. I flick the light to my register and wait until Barbara places her items on the conveyor belt. Barbara is an old lady who comes in every Monday around the same time to go grocery shopping.

"How are you, Barbara?"

"I'm fine." Her hands shake when she places the jars of pickles on the belt.

"Do you need help?"

"Oh, no. I got it," she says, waving me off.

Last time, she dropped the jar of pickles, and I couldn't get the smell of pickle juice off my hands for a week.

"How about to your car?" I ask, double-bagging the jars.

I wonder what she does with all the jars of pickles. I have scanned six this time. She usually buys three every week.

When she swipes her card, it doesn't go through. I cleared the payment so she could try again.

"I'm sorry, Ivy. I can't remember which card I used last time."

"It was a blue one."

"Is everything alright?" Kevin asks, standing way too close behind me. If I step back, I'll run into his stomach.

I smile at Barbara when she looks behind me. "Everything is fine," she replies, waving her crinkly hand. "Ivy was being a peach, helping me remember what card I used last time."

After a minute of watching her rummaging in her big bag, she finally pulls it out. Kevin reaches over to help her swipe her card instead of going around. His stomach presses into my side in the small space between the register and the scanner. His face is inches from my cheek. I try holding my breath so I don't smell the Old Spice mixed with the smell of an ashtray coming from his skin. His smell makes me want to puke.

I'm relieved when she swats his hand away with a huff. "I got it, Kevin. I'm old, but I still work." She swipes her card, and it goes through.

"You're all set, Barbara."

Kevin helps me bag the last of her items, prolonging the fact that he shouldn't be this close.

When she leaves, pushing the cart out of the exit, I can feel his cigarette breath on my neck. "You could ask me for help. I'll gladly give it to you, Ivy," he says, but I don't miss the innuendo on the last part. My creep-o-meter rises in warning.

"I didn't need any help," I counter. He grips both my

arms, and I give a little shrug, hoping he takes the hint to back off.

"Like I said, anytime," he says, sliding his hands down my arms while I breathe through my mouth. I sigh when he walks away.

I clear the register and mutter, "Creep."

After four hours of scanning customers' groceries, the last one walks through my lane. I press the button on the belt so the three items he usually gets reach the sensor. My shift is over in three minutes. I shut off the light, indicating that my lane is closed.

"You need a ride home?"

I look up at what I call my side hustle, scanning the energy drink and box of condoms with a pack of gum.

Dean Foster, the owner of Down to Flush, from next door. He is thirty-eight, not bad-looking, has no children, is not married, and fixes toilets for a living.

"Yeah," I mumble.

Girls like me don't have a choice. We have to survive somehow.

CHAPTER THREE

"ARCH YOUR BACK," Dean says, wrapping his fist around my blond hair.

I place my hands flat on the island in his kitchen, bent over the edge. My skirt is crudely shoved up my waist. I can feel the tip of his cock wrapped in the condom nudging my entrance. I close my eyes when he shoves his cock inside me, feeling his fingers gripping my hips with each thrust. I press my teeth on my bottom lip to keep it from trembling, trying to think of something else. Anything that will help me escape. I hate the burning sensation when he penetrates me because I can't get wet.

"There you go, baby. That's it. Give me that tight pussy," he says, followed by a grunt. His hot breath is on the back of my neck. He fucks me in rapid, measured thrusts for about a minute until he comes shuddering, gasping for air.

I ran into Dean at the grocery store when I argued with my mother about money on the phone. It was the summer before repeating my junior year. I had to tell Kevin I needed my hours cut short to finish school. I got a glimpse of my life working at the grocery store and figured without a high school diploma; my options were slim in getting out of Stockbridge. Dropping out wasn't an option.

Dean saw me walking across the parking lot and offered to give me a ride home. The sun was setting. It was getting dark, so I agreed. I agreed to more than that. A hundred bucks every time he would give me a ride home, and I would return the favor. I cried the first time when I got home after he fucked me, but I was relieved when I could pay the light bill.

Then it became a routine. He would come into the grocery store, buy a couple of things, never forgetting the condoms, and ask if I needed a ride home. He would bring me to his house four blocks away and fuck me on his kitchen island. With my school uniform on, always on weekdays, and always after my shift at the grocery store.

"Turn around."

He slides his cock out, and I wince from the sting. He disposes of the condom and watches me while he strokes himself. He slides on another condom. His brown hair is sticking up like he was running his fingers through it, standing naked in his kitchen.

Dean is six feet tall, lean with a flat stomach, a patch of hair on his chest, and brown eyes and hair. An average guy without a romantic bone in his body. He's rough like every man I have ever met. He makes me feel cheap and wants only one thing. To fuck me.

"Do you know how many guys who work for me want to fuck you?" He jerks his dick faster. I can see the red tip through the condom every time his hand goes up and down, trying to get it hard.

"Let me guess, all of them," I answer sarcastically.

He chuckles. "If they only knew I'm the one fucking that tight pussy."

How charming. He forgot to mention the one-minute warning.

"Lucky you."

"Let me see those pretty tits, Ivy."

I harden my jaw, looking at the cabinet behind him. I cup my tits, playing with my nipples so he can finish, and I can go home, take a shower, and find something to eat.

"Tell me you want me to fuck you, Ivy."

I found out why he's single. He comes before he even starts. He does this every time, trying to get his dick hard, stroking it like a fourteen-year-old. His skin is already clammy from the effort. The veins on his neck are sticking out. His face flushed red.

"I want you to fuck me," I say in a flat tone.

He licks his greedy lips. "Fuck, baby." He steps closer, but his dick is flaccid inside the condom, and it's about to slide off. Dean's cock is on the below-average side, but when it's soft, it's small.

My eyes slide up, his face beet red, and then he lets out a ragged breath. "Fuck!" he yells, causing me to jolt. I quickly shove my skirt down and button my shirt when he turns around, throwing the condom in the trash.

When he walks back, I'm ready to leave.

"I'm sorry." He shuffles on his feet. "I didn't mean to yell." He slides a sweater over his head. "It's not your fault. I'm stressed with work… you understand, right?"

I smooth my hair so I don't look like he fucked me in the back seat of a car when I get home. "It's fine."

He says the same thing all the time. It is always stress,

work, or whatever excuse he comes up with. He is single. His outbursts are also a little scary. I couldn't imagine what woman could deal with that if she dated him on top of his rough hands.

He pulls off the main highway in his white late model Dodge Ram pickup truck, stopping by the side stairwell. Checking the time on the big screen in the center console, it's nine-thirty.

"Here." He hands me a crisp one-hundred-dollar bill. "I won't be able to do this next week." My stomach bottoms out because I need the money. "I-I have a date with someone. I'm dating someone," he admits.

I turn my head, taking the money. "Okay." I jump out of his truck, shutting the door, dying to leave. He doesn't wait until I get up the stairs before he drives off. Asshole.

I stomp my way up the stairs, trying to figure out how to make up the money. I was making a hundred bucks about twice a week with Dean on top of the three hundred and eighty a month part-time at the grocery store after taxes. It gave me enough to help pay the utilities because I knew my mother wouldn't have it, plus the other half of the rent. We could barely afford groceries to last us until the next paycheck. Money for gas was another issue living in a small town where public transportation was limited. Compared to the city, gas in Stockbridge is expensive on top of the car insurance for the old piece of shit Oldsmobile my mother drives that's on its last leg. But she has money for cigarettes and who knows what else.

The apartment door to my right opens when I reach

the second floor. The stench of marijuana causes me to crinkle my nose.

"Hey, Ivy."

I look over at Scott—the Meadow apartment's pothead and drug dealer—leaning on the doorjamb. He's lighting a joint with a lighter that doesn't work every time he tries to turn it with his thumb.

"Getting the last hit for the night, Scott?"

"Want to take a hit?" he asks with a grin.

"I don't smoke. I gotta go. I have school in the morning."

Scott mostly deals with marijuana and cocaine. He sometimes sells Adderall and X, but he isn't a successful drug dealer. He always offers me something that is related to drugs, trying to lure me in. The phrase "don't get high on your own supply" doesn't apply to Scott. If he still lives here.

He finally gets the lighter to work and lights the joint, taking a drag. "When are you going to hang out with me? Every time I ask, you got an excuse."

"I'm busy," I reply, walking toward my front door and fishing out the key.

He wants me to get high with him, hoping we can hook up, and who knows what else he has in mind. I have enough problems.

"You're not busy right now," he says, echoing down the hall.

I turn the lock. "Good night, Scott." I shut the door, leaning against it. Why do guys have to be such creeps? It's not like I have a sign on my forehead that screams I'M A TARGET FOR ASSHOLES. TAKE ADVANTAGE OF ME.

CHAPTER FOUR

"I DON'T KNOW why you just don't ask for your hours back at the grocery store, Ivy."

I slam the refrigerator door closed. It doesn't rattle because nothing is inside except a tap water container, a ketchup bottle, and an empty juice carton.

"If I want to graduate this year and get my diploma, I can't do that working at the grocery store during school hours, Mom. I can't be at two places at the same time."

"Well, school isn't paying the bills. Is it?"

Her voice is getting worse with all the cigarettes she smokes. I have to air out the house and buy the bootleg Pine-Sol they sell at Dollar General so the house doesn't smell like a month-old ashtray.

"It will, once I graduate and can get a decent job. Not some minimum wage cashier position where the manager looks at me like he wants to take my clothes off and screw me on the register."

She laughs. Her teeth are a yellow shade like the ones you see in an eighties movie. All the actors in that era had stained yellow teeth, not the pearly whites you see on social media or the latest blockbuster when it hits theaters. It's a shame to see my mother like this. Her face is already showing signs of age, and she is only forty-four.

She has jowls, sagging skin on her jawline, and wrinkles over her top lip, made worse by smoking. Her hoarse voice doesn't help, and neither does the smell of cigarettes that clings to her skin. I remember her being pretty.

"You should fuck him. You're nineteen, you know," she says, with an unlit cigarette between her lips. She lights it and takes a drag. "He'll give you a raise."

I lean back on the Formica counter, bile rising in my throat when I imagine what Kevin would look like naked.

"That's gross. I can't believe you would say that."

"I did it. Your grandma did it," she admits. "You should be grateful I blessed you with platinum blond hair and a pair of nice tits to go with a nice perky round ass. You would be stupid not to use that to your advantage."

I have, and there is nothing useful about it. All it gets you is a hundred bucks, a load of shame, and a bag of self-esteem issues. I'll never tell her about Dean because that would make me like her. The last thing you want to do is become the thing you hate the most. A woman who has sex for money because she isn't good to be anything else. My mother dabbled in drugs, and all the smoking made her look older, and then, men stopped looking at her. She got a job wherever she could or whoever would hire her.

"That is not what I want, Mom. You would have never had to do that if you stayed in school and tried to do something with your life."

She snorts. "Sooner or later, you'll have no choice." Not wanting to hear more of this shit, I walk toward my room. "Walk away!" She raises her voice. "That's what you do best. Just like your father did when I told him I was pregnant with you. I had no choice but to do what I had to do to survive." I slam my bedroom door. "And neither will you!"

Why do parents expect their kids to follow in their footsteps? It's because their life is so shitty, they think that you can't do better. They expect you to follow the same narrative. In my case, white trash, raised in the trailer park with a dead-beat parent and an absent meth dealer for a father. Now my mother works as a server who fucks whoever for a price if given the opportunity. She has no education and no aspirations to do shit with her life.

After a cold shower, I lie naked on my bed. It's still hot the last week of August and running the air conditioner is not an option right now. I look at my phone, pulling up the Circle of Freaks paranormal circus website. Tickets are available every weekend until the first week of November. Then they head off to other states across the country. Tickets are for both Saturday and Sunday. Two shows that include access to all the rides at the Stockbridge fair. Price. Three hundred bucks a ticket plus tax. There is a pop-up that comes up.

ENTER TO WIN A FREE TICKET.

I read the fine print. No purchase is necessary. I click on it and enter my phone number, email, and address. What are the chances? Probably a million to one, but a girl could hope. The tickets sell out almost every weekend.

I've been fascinated with clowns and the circus since the age of eight. I thought it was cool and still do.

Some kids fear clowns and creepy masks, but I never

did. I love the makeup, the acrobats, the illusionists, and the breathtaking acts. When the paranormal circus became popular, it was a twist that took the audience into a darker world.

When I was in middle school, I imagined being part of a circus. I wanted to dress up like a clown for Halloween every year. When Stephen King's *It* came out, I checked it out of the library and read it. It was good, and I couldn't put it down. When the movie came out, I couldn't watch it because my mother said she would not pay for me to watch a bunch of kids afraid of a stupid clown. If I wanted to see it that bad, I should wait until I could get it for free.

I had to kiss Brandon Smith in seventh grade to get a copy. It was like kissing a wet fish.

Sometimes, the drive-in theater, around Halloween, plays *It* on the screen. I climb up on the roof of the apartment building to see it from the north side. The trees on that side haven't grown high enough to block the view.

I scroll through my photos of screenshots of different acts and clowns I found online. The women look spectacular and sexy in their outfits, and the men in their costumes with face paint. The paranormal cirque is like an R-rated movie. The traditional circus in the US began in Philadelphia and was first introduced in the eighteen hundreds by the Ringling Brothers. I heard in Stock-bridge that a fair started around the same time and is still here. Then, the circus was added, and it was called the Circle of Freaks.

When the paranormal circus became popular around Halloween, it became the year's event for the last twenty years. Every weekend, late August through the first week of November, the circus comes to where it all began. Two years ago, they introduced the haunted carnival that surrounds the circus to attract more visitors. But no one talks about what goes on inside the tent. No one.

In my sophomore year, I was obsessed with finding everything there was to know about the Circle of Freaks. I asked around, searched online, but found nothing except a review that said it was scary as fuck and awesome. All that did was make me want to see it even more.

AFTER LOCKING up and eating what was left of the dry cereal, I make my way past Scott's apartment with GOT WEED? spray-painted next to his front door, each letter in the colors of the rainbow. Whoever did it must think Scott is gay because right at the bottom, it reads FAGGOT offensively. He probably pissed off someone last night. It's quiet coming from his apartment. He must be passed out from all the drugs and weed he consumes. On the weekends, beginning on Fridays, he gets more visitors than a public bathroom at all hours of the night.

When I make it to school, I notice more flyers for the fair. These are geared more toward the circus and the haunted carnival. CARNEVIL in big black and red letters with the Circle of Freaks logo and a circus tent on the bottom.

"Hey, Freak?"

Turning around, I watch Alice walk from the student parking lot, ignoring Jason. He's sitting with a bunch of cheerleaders and most of the football team.

His gaze follows her until she is almost about to pass me. Then he spots me. *Great.* Better me than her, I guess.

"Hey, Ivy. Do you and the freak want to suck me off after school?" I roll my eyes and tilt my head. "I thought we talked about this, Jason. It's too small." The stupid smile on his face drops when everyone around him begins to laugh.

"That's because a slut like you needs to have a huge cock to stuff inside that loose pussy. We've been over this."

To my surprise, Alice flips him off before heading into the main building. Her long straight dark hair covers the side of her face like a curtain.

"Anytime, Freak." He gets up from the bench. "I'll even throw in a pity fuck while you watch your whore of a friend Ivy when she takes my cock."

Jason is an insufferable pig who loves to treat girls like shit. He thinks because his father owns a Mercedes Benz dealership that he's hot shit. Some girls might find him funny or get turned on. Or that he drives a Mercedes GT and has Daddy's money, but not me and Alice.

"Hey, Jason?" He looks up. "Good luck finding your dick." I turn around, ignoring his last jab.

"It's right here, you desperate slut. Tommy told us what a greedy little whore you are."

He left out the part where he came in less than two minutes but whatever. I've had enough of Jason for the day.

I catch up to Alice walking down the hall through the

throng of bodies. "Hey, thanks." She keeps walking until she stops at her locker and turns her head to look at me. "For what you did back there. I'm not what they say I am."

Not intentionally.

She nods. "I know."

I raise my brows in surprise. "You do?"

She slides the textbook for the class we have together out of her locker. "You went out with Tommy on a date after he kept asking you your sophomore year. I was a freshman, but everyone knew you went out with him that one time. He made sure everyone knew you slept with him and made-up crap slut shaming you. That's what guys do when they see a girl, and they know she doesn't feel the same. You found him lame, and it's obvious you don't like him." She shuts her locker and spins the dial. "That doesn't make you a slut. Besides, I have never seen you with another guy since my freshman year. Not one."

I wish I could tell her she is right. In the traditional sense, I haven't. But I'm not sure anymore, not after my thing with Dean.

"I don't think you're a freak."

She grins. "Thanks, I guess."

I heard Alice lives in an abandoned estate on Avirce St. surrounded by miles of trees. Her mother talked to the school counselor, and word got around that she takes medication to help her cope. Some crap about her seeing and hearing things that aren't there. I have never seen her act weird at school. In the same way, I've never seen her around any friends. Alice keeps to herself and avoids everyone like I do. We both have that in common.

"I guess we both have something in common," I say, walking alongside her toward class.

She pinches her brows. "What's that?"

"We both have people saying things about us that are untrue."

We walk in class, and she actually smiles. She takes her usual seat in the back of the class. When she smiles, it makes her even more beautiful. She has dark lashes that frame her pretty brown eyes with a natural arch to her brows. She has a small, straight nose and full-shaped lips.

"I agree," she says, "It's when we believe what they say that it becomes a problem."

I stare at the old wooden desk in my seat with IVY IS A SLUT carved on the surface. She's right. That's when you begin to lose yourself. When you believe what people assume they know about you.

CHAPTER FIVE

THE BUS DROPS ME OFF, and I head toward the Big H for my shift. I ignore Kevin when I walk in to change and his eyes remain stuck below the hem of my skirt. My mother's words last night mess with my head, making me feel worse than I already do. At least she said she paid the light. That means I can help with the other half of the rent, and I need not worry about Dean.

Since repeating my junior year in high school, forty times I let him fuck me on his kitchen island before he took me home. Last night had been the first time he told me he couldn't take me home because he had a date or was dating someone. I hadn't given it much thought if it was dating or not. In those moments before I shut down, all I could think about was if he was wearing a condom. Like my past, he's a secret I want no one to know about. Because that would make what the kids called me at school true and prove my mother right.

It's not that I'm hung up about it. I used to be, but you can only cry so many tears. Soon enough, they dry up. I couldn't do anything about it. I had no one except my mother and nowhere to go. It was the only way I could stay in school. Some kids hate having to go to school and take living in a stable home for granted. They always complain, preferring to skip class for the mall or the lake to screw around, get high, and fuck. I was groomed to sleep with men for money. I had to fuck for a buck to stay in school. It was a transaction. I always told myself it could be worse. Dean could expect more from me.

When I was thirteen, I didn't understand why men looked at me funny. I understood the day my mother brought a man to the house. He made me go down on him when my mother left for the store. I threw up, and he hit me across the face. He made me clean it up and shoved his dick in my mouth. He told me he couldn't wait until I was older. The school saw the cut and bruise on my face and called social services. My mother said I fell off my bike, and they bought it. When it happened a second time, she pulled me out of school, and we moved here.

I watch the belt run with two bags of chips, two cans of Coke, and a Hershey bar.

"Oh my God, she works here?" I look up to see Emma, captain of the cheerleading team, and Tommy Hill. She stifles a laugh when I scan the items and place them in a grocery bag.

"Did you know she worked here? Is that why you brought me here instead of the gas station down the road?"

I ignore them, smacking my stale bubble gum, blowing a small bubble, and scanning the cans of soda.

"I didn't know she worked here," Tommy replies.

Liar. He knows I work here. He came in a bunch of times in the summer on Sundays with his mother. He knows where I live too. He knows more than he should.

When I look up, Tommy is standing behind Emma. Since he's above six feet, he takes advantage. His eyes focus on my shirt, where the button causes a small hole, and you can see my bra.

I pop the bubble and twirl my tongue around, dragging it in my mouth. "Will that be all?" I ask.

He tears his eyes away. "Wait," he says, rushing to the pharmacy aisle and coming back with a pack of condoms.

Emma smirks at me, sliding her arm around Tommy's waist. If she only knew I don't give a shit. If she only knew she was doing me a favor.

I scan the box of condoms, dropping it into the bag with the potato chips. "Will that be all for you both today?" I ask with a smile.

"Yes," Tommy says stiffly.

"That will be… eighteen dollars and fifty-five cents."

I can't say I'm surprised when Emma pulls out a twenty and pays. I give her the change, sliding the bags over to her. "You both have a nice rest of your day."

She takes the bags. "Have fun bagging groceries," she quips.

"Make sure you get your three condoms worth," I shoot back. More like three minutes' worth since she paid for the guy's snacks and condoms. He didn't offer to chip in at least.

Her face falls, and Tommy stands there without a word instead of defending her. She glances at him, his light green eyes staring at me for a second too long. "I knew it!" She screeches and storms off with the bags in her hands.

"You should go after your girlfriend."

"She's not my girlfriend."

I pick up the cleaning spray bottle and paper towel and clean the scanner, hoping he can see the disgust on my face. "Will people slut-shame her tomorrow as they did me since she isn't your girlfriend?" He turns around and walks out.

Bastard.

The next day at school, I had my answer. No one mentioned Tommy and Emma ever going out. They didn't call her an easy lay or a slut. He didn't spread rumors about her. He also didn't stop the one he created about me, either.

Sometimes, I wonder what I did to deserve it. I would ask myself if that was what people saw in me, especially men. Did they know my mother had loose morals, and by default, it made me like her? I gave no reason for anyone to think that about me when I moved here. Unless they found out about Dean. But that would make him an asshole for paying for it, and it was never something I wanted to do. I knew I had no choice, but I had a goal.

I'm bagging the last of the customer's groceries. Clear the register and mindlessly begin scanning the next items without looking up. But when I hear a familiar name coming from a woman, I pause.

"I don't like those, Dean. The almond ones are better," the woman whines, placing a bag of chocolate almonds on the belt. She isn't wrong; they are better.

But what has me angry when I look up is Dean's smug face. It's not that he's dating someone, but that he brought her here out of all places. First Tommy yesterday, and now him. What the hell? And with Sarah? I know her because she works at the only insurance office by the mall. She's in her late twenties. Brown hair, and eyes, and is skinny. Not what you would consider pretty because her nose is too big for her face and her clothes sag on her frame. Her yellow sundress reminds me of a mannequin when you try to fit it into a dress that is too big.

It's not that I'm bothered he's dating her, but it's a dick move knowing I work here and to come into my lane —selfish prick. Why do guys get a kick out of doing that? Is it because they lack where it matters? They treat women like shit but love to call themselves a man.

I can feel Dean staring, but I do my job as a cashier, scanning and bagging the items. I smile at Sarah when she walks down the lane past the payment system.

"How are you, Sarah? You probably don't remember me," I say, watching Dean shift uncomfortably with his feet.

"You're Maggy Sloan's daughter, right?"

"Yep."

"I remember now. I sold your mom the policy for her car, and you came in with her."

"That's right."

"Isn't a small world?"

I glance at Dean. "It is. You never know who you might run into these days."

"You must run into Dean all the time since his business is right next door."

I glance back at her, ignoring the way his fists clench, and reply, "Once a week at least."

"We ran into each other the same way you and your mom did," she gushes. "We've been dating for about two weeks now."

What a lying sack of shit.

I plant a fake smile after ringing them up. He slides his card harder than necessary and waits for the machine to approve the transaction. It spits the receipt. I don't miss the anger he is trying to hide, but I'm relieved. My idea of sex was never to get paid for it, and if my circumstances were different, I would have told Dean to fuck off.

I hand him the receipt with a grin. "I wish you both the best."

Her cheeks bloom. "Thank you."

The way Dean is quiet and looking straight ahead, I doubt he feels the same way.

CHAPTER SIX

BY THE TIME my shift ended, it was late. I had to help stock different grocery items in my lane. When Dean didn't take me home the rest of the week, I took the shuttle to the mall. It was better than walking the three miles on the main highway to get home. The shuttle bus at least had air-conditioning and so did the mall, which made the trip easier.

Instead of walking across the parking lot to get to my building, I would walk inside and out of the back exit. I also got to window shop. I have always loved the smell that comes from the different spaces compared to the apartment. It smells like new clothes and different fragrances. Like the perfume samples from the magazines you find in the mail. I couldn't afford anything, but it was still nice to look at what was trending.

I make my way to the stop where the shuttle picks up people trying to get to the mall and check the time on my phone. It's already eight thirty, so I missed the last shuttle for the day. The mall would be closed and the last movie at the drive-in theater during the weekday would have started.

My mother doesn't get off for another four hours, and she can't afford to step out of work to take me home.

I have no other choice but to walk the three miles home. It's dark, the sun has set, and I have fifty percent battery life on my cell phone.

The clouds move heavily across the moon. The main highway is a two-way street with no sidewalk and woods surrounding the side. Every so often, the smell of roadkill would hit me.

Occasionally, you would see cars speed by, and some would slow down. My heart would beat fast inside my chest, fear gripping me in its fist. All I could think about was to run into the woods and hide if it stopped.

The grass reaches my ankles, brushing my sweaty skin. It was hot today when the sun was out, but as the night settled in, I could feel the slight breeze from the wind cooling my skin. The trees sway, causing the leaves to float to the ground. The smell of fall floats in the air.

I look to my left and my right when I hear a noise coming from deep in the woods. I drag my finger across the screen of my phone, pressing my thumb on the flashlight and hoping it's not a bear.

Bears in Stockbridge are a problem. They can come out of the woods when looking for food, and right now, I look like their next meal.

"Hey, you need a ride?"

A gray minivan with fingerprint smudges on the window pulls up and reminds me of the moms who come to the Big H with their kids screaming because they won't share the bag of snacks they opened before they were paid for.

A couple about the same age as my mother pulls up beside me, giving me a warm smile. There is a collection of items hanging from their rearview mirror—graduation tassels, a collection of air fresheners, beaded neck-laces, and a rosary.

The man reaches over the woman in the passenger seat with a Boston Celtics hat that obscures most of his face.

"It's dangerous to be walking on a road like this. The cars drive by fast, and bears come out of the woods around this time of year. Do you live nearby?"

My unease blankets my chest, cursing myself for staying later than I needed to. "Thanks… but…my boyfriend is picking me up." I check my phone. "He should be here any minute.

"Alright, you be careful now," the woman says with a baleful grin.

The window rolls up, and the van pulls away, leaving me with a sense of dread.

When the taillights are like red beacons in the distance, I run toward the tree line, but a loud horn blaring behind me causes me to turn. I let out a sigh of relief when I recognized Alice's car.

She rolls her window down. "You need a ride?"

I nod. "Yes, Alice. Thank God." I run up to her Tesla and get in.

"Is everything alright? You look like you've been running from Jason Voorhees."

"Close. This couple stopped to offer me a ride, and something was off. I told her my boyfriend was going to pick me up, and the way she smiled before they pulled away gave me the creeps. All the talk about teenage girls missing has me thinking everyone is a body snatcher."

"That must have been really scary. It's dark out." She looks up through the moon roof. "The moon is full. You know what they say, weird people come crawling out when the moon is full."

I look around at the simple but high-tech car. "Thank you for stopping. Nice car, by the way. The handles are bitch to figure out, though."

"Trust me, it's not nice when you have to wait inside to charge it when the battery runs low after driving in it all day. I'm lucky it's charged every morning because I forget. I think it's my mother or stepfather who remembers or I wouldn't make it to school. They keep giving me shit all the time."

"Mine can't make rent." I point at my uniform shirt with the Big H and name tag. "It's why I'm walking home. I had to stay late and missed the shuttle."

She pulls out onto the road. A bell chimes from the screen, flashing that she is going the wrong way, but she continues in the opposite direction.

"I had to get out of my house. My parents don't want me out, but I couldn't take it any more so I snuck out."

"Have you been to the haunted fair?"

"I'm not allowed to go. My mother and my therapist don't think it's a good idea. Too much stimulation."

I snort. "What do they say about sex? That's stimulation."

Alice laughs. "I asked if I could have a boyfriend, and they said they didn't think that was a good idea either."

"What? Are they going to send you to a convent or something?"

"Doubt it. They might think I'll come out like that diabolical nun in the movie."

I don't want to ask what they say she has because Alice looks normal. I see no signs of crazy. Unlocking my phone and scrolled to the last website I was browsing to see if they've announced the winner for the ticket giveaway.

"Are you going?" she asks, glancing at the Circle of Freaks page.

"I want to, but it costs three hundred bucks. I make that in a month working at the grocery store, but I need it to help my mother with rent. I signed up to see if I could win a free ticket on the website." I'm short even with what I make in the grocery store, but I don't tell her that.

"I heard if you go to the haunted fair during the week and you're wearing an eighteen and over orange band, they hand out free tickets."

"Really?" I ask excitedly. "How do you know that?"

"I heard Mich from the football team tell Jason. I think they were going since they turned eighteen."

I search for free tickets for the Circle of Freaks circus and bingo. "He's right. There's a blog. It says the Circle of Freaks will hand out a few tickets to fairgoers if they enter the haunted carnival during the week."

"You want to go that bad?"

I glance at her. "Yeah, I've loved the circus since I was a kid and figured I was too old to go, but this one… this one I really want to check out."

She drums her black-painted fingernails on the steering wheel like she's contemplating. She slows down, turns the wheel, and drives in the opposite direction right before she reaches the apartment complex.

I point with my thumb over my shoulder. "That was my stop?"

She grins and says, "I know." She presses the search icon on the gigantic screen that looks like an iPad and types in Carnevil. The address pops up, routing the car to the destination and letting her know how much battery she has left.

"The ticket to the haunted fair is twenty-eight dollars, and it includes all the rides. I could loan you the money."

I have the hundred I got from Dean.

"Thank you, but I have enough." I look down at the vest, take it off, stuff it into my bag, and fix my hair.

"You never know. Maybe you'll get lucky. Even if you don't, you'll have fun trying. The circus tent shouldn't be far. No one knows what goes on inside unless you pay to go."

"Tell me about. I think it's why I want to go so bad."

"You like the dark paranormal circus stuff?"

I shrug. "Yeah, why not? Beats the hell out of work, school, and where I live."

"Trust me, I know the feeling."

I wonder what she means by that, but I don't ask.

CHAPTER SEVEN

THE MOON IS DROOPED low in the pitch-black sky, and a quiet, cool breeze blows through the amusement park. The haunted side of the carnival looks abandoned compared to the traditional one. A yin to the yang. There are screams on one side and laughter on the other. Like two dimensions.

We walk up to the dilapidated entryway, the lights flick to life, throwing shadows over the rusted ticket booths. An old, tattered sign reads "Welcome to Carnevil: Where Fear Meets Fun."

A chill mixed with fear and excitement grips me at the thought of promise. I spot people from school and a bunch of kids who looked like they were in middle school.

We make the line far enough to the left to avoid being spotted by anyone from school.

"Are you sure you won't get in trouble for bringing me here?" I ask.

"I don't think my parents will notice me gone. I closed the garage so they thought my car was inside. My stepfather is usually away on business, and my mother is fast asleep. How about you?"

"My mom couldn't give a shit as long as I come up with the other half of the rent."

We step forward to the front of the line. "That bad, huh?"

I scoff. "You have no idea."

The Ferris wheel is the focal point in the center when we hand our tickets to the guy at the ticket booth. Skeletal figures are seated in the creaking gondolas with bony fingers. The wheels spin with unnatural speed. The riders' laughter turns to terrified screams. It is obvious they made the Ferris wheel look haunted for added effect.

We both jolt when a sinister clown pops out of nowhere through the fog. His grin wide, and his teeth gleam with malevolence.

"Come, play with me," he hisses, beckoning us to come over.

We keep walking. Masked characters pop out from hidden spaces.

The cotton candy vendor holds up what looks like blood-red wisps and hisses, "Hungry."

The cotton candy he held dripped dark red to look like fresh blood. The popcorn in the cart looked flavored with a hint of something unsettling. Vendors with face paint are on each side in decorated sinister-looking carts.

I glance at Alice, her body tense and eyes wide as she takes it all in. The makeup on each of the actor's faces looks like they spent hours applying it. I wonder how they can keep up with it every night.

We reach the ride section of the fair. The rides are designed to fit the theme. The Roller Coaster of Evil is a rickety, rust-covered monstrosity that appears on the verge of collapse. It races through dark tunnels with flickering lights. There is a sudden drop that plunges into total darkness. Sinister laughter echoes throughout the air, leaving you with a sense of upcoming dread. Then comes the laughter. People get off with smiles on their faces from the thrill.

"Do you want to ride, Alice?" I hold up my left hand, flashing her my orange band we got from the ticket booth. "We can ride everything," I say with a smile. "Let's have fun."

We stand in line after dodging a couple of creepy nuns popping out to scare us with upside-down crosses hanging from their necks. My stomach hardens, and my palms sweat, anticipating the roller coaster and how fast it dips on the track.

"Alright, fuck it. How bad could it be?" she says and looks over. "Are they letting the people in costumes ride with random people?"

I follow her line of sight. A bunch of actors from the scare zones are getting on the ride. Some wear masks, and some wear makeup. They are walking like a group of killers in the movie *The Purge*. Only actors who work for the fair are allowed to wear masks and costumes. I didn't miss the big red sign with a line across that read,

NO MASKS ALLOWED

"Yeah."

"That's…crazy."

I turn when I hear a scream. " This place is crazy," I mutter.

A tall figure in the center of the group with a black cross painted on his white mask grabs my attention. He jumps over the railing like he does it all the time. As we walk closer to get in line, he's even taller. His shoulders are broad, and his back is massive. You can tell by the way his muscles move under the black fabric.

"Whoa." Alice leans close when she notices him. "Where did he come from?"

I look over my shoulder and see where the rest of the group is walking away from a blocked area that reads, MORE BLOOD THIS WAY and CIRCLE OF FREAKS PARANORMAL CIRCUS.

I grin. "They're part of the circus." I point behind her. "They came from over there."

Alice cranes her neck. "You're right."

The line moves, and we're next to ride. I tug Alice forward. My pulse pounds when I see the masked actors slide inside random carts.

"Have fun dying," one of them jeers.

A woman dressed like an erotic circus performer wears fishnets under a short skirt and boots stopping mid-thigh. She has fake blood dripping over the swell of her breasts.

"I'm hungry," she says, baring her teeth. "Women are my favorite. So soft." She tilts her head and says absent-mindedly, "So pretty." She licks her blood-painted lips.

She jerks her head and straightens when the guy in front of us sits inside the cart. "He'll do," she says, sliding next to him. The poor guy's eyes widen in terror. She tilts her head back and laughs when the ride attendant secures the lap bar.

I smile. "She's awesome," I say, mindlessly sliding inside the next cart.

I'm startled when a dark hooded figure slides in next

to me instead of Alice. It's the man with the white mask and an upside-down cross painted in the center. He angles his head slowly and places a gloved finger over his masked lips, silently telling me not to scream. He's so tall, his knees are bent uncomfortably, making it difficult for the lap bar to close.

I try to keep calm.

I crane my neck to see Alice seated with another man wearing a hooded cloak with a black mask that looks like it's made of carbon fiber. Alice stares straight ahead, her shoulders tense. Her knuckles are white from gripping the bar. The ride operator checks each lap bar beginning with the back carts.

When I face forward, I let out a yelp. The man is looking straight at me. I can't see his eyes, but I can hear his muffled breathing.

The ride attendant gets to our cart and reaches over to pull the bar near my hand. I pull my skirt down the tops of my thighs for modesty, wishing I'd worn pants. A gloved hand shoots out, snatching the operator's hand in a tight grip and shoving it off.

"Just checking it," the ride operator says nervously with both hands raised. He glances at me. "Making sure you're safe."

He walks away toward the operator booth. He flicks a couple of switches.

When the ride lurches forward, people scream prematurely in excitement. The tension builds as the coaster moves higher with every *clank-clank-clank* from the chain mixed with the rush of fear and exhilaration.

A surge of electricity shoots up my arm when his gloved hand laces his fingers through mine.

People continue to scream behind us, but it fades as we reach the crest. Everything becomes clear for a few seconds. The lights, the crisp air, screaming, people running through the scare zones, and the smell of fair food.

Then, one by one, the cars fall down the track, eliciting bone-shilling screams.

The coaster stops right before the drop. I grip his hand tighter, thankful that it's there.

"Shit," I mumble.

My heart continues to beat hard in my chest, waiting for my stomach to drop. I can feel his gaze on me like fire over my skin.

A shrill laugh comes from the giant clown mask on top with flashing red eyes. The sound of screams pierces through the air. My hair blows from the wind. I look over, and my eyes widen when the first cart drops. I scream, and my body slams against his. He slides his arm around my shoulders, holding me close. I breathe in his rich scent of citrus and cedar, close my eyes, and feel how hard his muscles are underneath his costume. The man is solid. He must be one of the main circus performers. From what I've seen online, they have amazing physiques.

The coaster jerks with each turn, but he holds me against him. I squeeze my thighs together, arousal blooming between my thighs, not wanting him to let go. I've never had a man hold me like this—like I was his.

The coaster comes to a stop. He lets me go, the lap bar pulls up automatically, and he slides out of the cart. The loss of his heat causes me to shiver.

I follow everyone out the exit, looking for Alice, a little dazed. I finally spot her.

"Alice." I wave over.

She turns around. "That was insane," she says, but I don't miss the worried look crossing her features.

"Are you okay?"

She nods. "Yeah," she says, looking around.

I bet she's looking for the guy who rode with her because I can't find the one who sat next to me. They disappeared into thin air once we got off the ride.

"Did that guy say anything to you?" I ask.

"Not a word. He… sat there. He made sure I didn't jerk around, so that was a relief. I'm not sure, but if we rode together, we would have flown out of the cart. It was so fast."

I laugh. "I thought my heart was going to pop out of my chest when the ride stopped, and the clown started laughing."

We walk over to a guy wearing a costume with his face painted like a jester holding a red drink with smoke floating around the rim.

"Want some blood?" he asks with a sinister smile.

"How much is the blood?" I ask with a grin.

He looks behind us, his sinister grin falling off. Alice and I turn around, but all we see are people rushing by, screaming.

When we look back, the guy hands us two drinks. "Have a bloody night and be careful… you never know what can follow you."

"Funny." Alice grabs a drink and takes a sip.

I watch her face light up. "It's good." And she takes a bigger sip.

I try mine, and she is not wrong. It tastes like red fizzy soda. I hand him a ten-dollar bill, but he shakes his head and looks away. "How much for the drinks?"

His eyes are black from his contacts, but he doesn't respond and ignores us.

"Fine." I'm not going to turn down a free soda.

I look around for my masked guy but can't find him.

"Funny finding you here?" I whirl around, almost spilling my drink, to see Jason, Matt, Tommy from the football team, and Emma with a couple of girls from school. "You two a thing now? You know, we don't mind a little lesbian action."

"Fuck off."

"Fuck I can do, baby. You name the time and place, and I'll slide right in," Jason says, stepping closer.

"Oh, you finally found your dick?"

"You want me to show you, Ivy?" His eyes fall to my chest. "Do you want to see how big my dick is so you can ride it? I promise to make you scream louder than any ride here."

I don't miss the lust in his eyes.

"Let it go, Jason. Stop fucking around," Tommy scolds.

But he isn't. All he needs is the right push, and I have a strong feeling Jason is the type who wouldn't accept the word no.

In his mind, I'm easy and considered a slut. No one would believe me if he touched me without my consent, and he's preying on it.

I'm so sick of these assholes.

"I don't do kiddie rides, Jason. I like real men." I glance at Tommy. "The kind who finish the job."

"Spoken like the true slut that you are," Tommy sneers.

Emma sniggers. "You're such a ho."

"At least I don't pay for a guy's condoms so he can fuck me. Tell me, Emma. How was your three minutes in hell?" Her mouth falls open like a fish.

Emma thought she got a winner in Tommy, only to find out that he's a three-minute hit and quit.

Jason's lips twitch. "I can go all night."

"Pfft. Yeah, annoying everyone." I walk away with Alice in tow and mutter, "Prick."

"They're insufferable. All those guys do is think with their dicks. It's all that asshole Jason talks about."

"That's because he can't get laid."

"Is it true?" she asks. I pause in front of the trail leading to the haunted houses. "What you said about Tommy?"

"Yep." I sigh. "Awful. I didn't feel it, and it was my first time. He lasted three minutes. I counted." We step closer and get into the line to the first haunted house. "I faked it," I say with a laugh. "Then he called me a slut."

I'm relieved she doesn't ask if I've gone out with anyone else—if I had sex with anyone else. I prefer to omit than deny. I've never seen Alice with a boyfriend, but she mentioned her parents didn't think it was a good idea.

CHAPTER EIGHT

WE TOSS our drinks in the trash before we enter the haunted house. My eyes try to adjust to the darkness inside. Noises of doors opening and closing in the distance. Screams floating from deep inside.

Footsteps shuffle in the next room, followed by screams and then the sound of a chainsaw. Chills snake down my legs. There are beds with props of human bodies cut open with their insides hanging out.

We take small steps through the maze of the hallway. Alice screams when a guy with a deformed mask jumps out, and bumps into the wall. He looks grotesque and is making inhuman noises.

Doors slam ahead.

We laugh after we scream when another one pops out, making a weird animal noise.

We continue the labyrinth through the hallway, trying to find the exit when the floor gives way. I try to hold on to Alice when she shrieks before we plunge into a dark underground space.

"Alice!" I shout, looking around, but it's pitch black

with minimal light coming from the wooden slats of the walls.

"Alice!" I call out, but nothing.

Anxiety sets in when I cannot find an exit. *"Aaaaaaalice…. Aaaaalice. Are you there?"* Someone calls in an unnerving voice, reminding me of a horror movie.

"Who's there?" I ask.

I move to the left, trying to find the exit, when a mechanical monster rises from the ground with glowing red eyes, startling me. I run the other way when mechanical hands pop out followed by an ominous laugh. I try to scream, but I don't have enough air in my lungs and run into something hard. I look up, trying to focus, and notice someone tall in the dim light.

When it steps forward, I recognize the same guy who sat next to me on the roller coaster wearing the white mask.

I step back and sigh in relief. "It's you." He angles his head like a masked murderer. "Real funny. Can you help me get out of here and find my friend? We got separated when the trapdoor gave way, and I can't find the exit."

He shakes his head and slides a finger down the center of my neck, causing a ripple of fear to curl around my gut. There is no reason to be scared. People who work for the carnival don't harm the guests, but they don't usually touch them either.

I take another step back and hit a wall. He steps forward, closing the distance.

"What are you doing? I ask in a shaky voice.

He leans close. His mask touches my cheek.

"Shh…" His finger descends from the center of my

neck to my collarbone, then lower, fingering the button on my white blouse in circles. "Mm…" I close my eyes.

I should scream, but I can't do it.

His finger glides to the swell of my breast, then back up to my neck. My eyes fly open. Something warm is on my thigh, but I can't see clearly. I can feel him towering over me, swallowing me whole.

I'm frozen in place when his hand slides up my thigh.

"Please," I plead, but I don't know if I want him to stop or keep going.

I'm fucked up. That must be it. I'm not normal. A sane person screams. A sane person would push him away and fight him off. But I'm not sane. I'm fucking crazy and desperate for him to keep going. To keep touching me in the way I craved to be touched.

The friction builds between my legs, wanting him there. He slides his gloved hand higher on my thigh. Close, but not close enough to give me what I want. I grip his hard shoulders. A tingles slither through my fingers.

Logic rattles my brain, and I push him away. "Let me out!"

He drops his hands and steps away toward the other side of the room, then pushes the door open like it appeared from thin air.

I checked everywhere, and there wasn't a way out. The light from the carnival rides guides me out, and I run. I look left and right, following the way out. The smell of popcorn hits me with the sound of a bell ringing from a game. I glance behind me to see if he followed me.

"Ivy?" I turn and sigh in relief when Alice runs up to

me. "I've been trying to find you. I looked everywhere. Are you okay? You look flushed."

It's not from fear. I'm turned on by the man wearing a white mask and black costume.

"I was trying to find a way out. I called out for you, but you didn't respond. It was dark, and it took me a bit to find a way out."

"Did a guy in a mask show up and freak you out?" she asks.

"Yeah. You?"

She has an uncertain look in her eyes. "The same one from the roller-coaster ride?"

"I think we better call it a night."

"Yeah," she agrees. "This place is crazy."

"Now I know why they're strict about the age limit." I slide my hand through her elbow and walk toward the exit. "Come on, I need to get home. I've had enough for one night."

The fog is thick. The machines on each side shoot more like thick clouds. I can't see the ticket booths by the exit. The smoke makes it hard to see the deeper you walk. I can feel Alice tense, her arm pressed around mine, expecting something to pop out and scare us.

We're about to reach the exit when the man wearing the white mask appears again. I ignore him this time and walk out of the way.

He steps in front of me at a safe distance and gives me a theatrical bow. You can tell he's mastered it and has done it a million times. He's holding a ticket in his outstretched hand. Butterflies swarm in my stomach, and I remember his fingers on my skin.

"Oh my God," I whisper softly when I see it.

I look at Alice.

"Take it, Ivy. He chose you," she says, urging me on. "Don't think about it and just…take it."

I've been waiting years to see a live circus and almost two to see the Circle of Freaks.

I grip the ticket. He raises his head for a second and kisses the top of my hand. The ticket is the only thing keeping our fingers from touching. It's not a kiss from his lips because of the mask, but it's hot.

When he finally releases the ticket, I say softly, "Thank you."

A clown hobbles over with big red shoes and fake blood dripping down his multicolored outfit. His clown makeup has a deadly twist. The corners of his mouth are painted upward in a grotesque parody of mirth, revealing yellow teeth that are jagged and irregular. It creates a nightmarish contrast to a clown's pleasant appearance. The teeth seem more like a predator's, ready to sink into prey. His smile is wide, stretching from ear to ear. It seems to defy the limits of human facial anatomy with lips that are a sickly shade of crimson.

"Thank you… for playing with us tonight," the clown says in a screechy voice. "We're DYING to have you come back." His cold and calculating eyes slide over me. "We can play a game… if you want. Do you like games?"

I step back. "T-that depends," I stammer.

Malevolent intent emanates from his eyes. They seem to pierce into my soul like he knows my deepest fears and darkest secrets.

"On what?"

I'm annoyed with myself for stammering like a nervous idiot. He's a man in a costume.

"How it ends."

"Come back and find out," he quips.

My masked performer straightens to his full height. Tall and commanding. Compared to the clown's average height, he seems taller than six foot three at least. The clown cowers dramatically, but I could see genuine fear in the clown's eyes.

"Come on," Alice says, tugging me toward the exit. "They're just messing "

But I'm not convinced. Right before we exit, I look over my shoulder, and the man with the white mask watches me while the fog whirls behind him. Behind the facade of fun, a darkness radiates within him that is terrifying.

CHAPTER NINE

DRACO

"I-I DIDN'T MEAN to frighten her, but she came to a haunted carnival," Levi says, pulling off his wig and clown shoes.

I tear my mask off my head and follow him inside the tent we use to change between shows. When he turns around, I wrap my hand around his throat, watching his eyes bulge—pure fear washing over his features.

"It's not that you frightened her, it's what you said and how you said it," I snarl. "The only one who can frighten her is me." I squeeze harder, watching his makeup crack. The skin around his pathetic smile is almost corpse-like. A contrast to the splatter of blood on my skin from my last victim. "The only game she plays is mine."

His hand tries to free the grip I have around his throat, but I'm taller and stronger than him. I find his attempt amusing. Levi has a problem switching off when he's in character. In this case, with her.

My phone vibrates in my pocket.

I broaden my smile. "You're lucky I'm expecting a phone call. If what you said causes her not to come back, start thinking about how you want to die." I release him, watching him fall on his ass while clutching his neck and gasping for air. I'm not sentimental, but she's different. I don't know why, but she is.

L: Thank you. She's home.

Draco: Who's the blonde?

L: Friend from school.

Draco: I want her.

L: It's not that simple.

Draco: Then I'll see how simple I can make it.

L: She's not what you're used to.

Draco: No one is, but that is beside the point. I want her.

L: Don't cause problems for me.

Draco: Is she yours? How old?

L: You know better than to ask me stupid questions. Nineteen.

Draco: Then what's the problem? I want to play.

L: Catching feelings?

Draco: Not my style, but I'll keep out of your way.

L: You're not the only one.

Draco: I'm not following.

L: Who is interested in her.

Draco: I'll make her choose, but I have a feeling she'll like it when I make her scream.

CHAPTER TEN

THE TICKET he gave me is different from the one sold online. It allows me free entry to the haunted carnival and circus. It also includes VIP seating at the show. It's even better than buying a ticket. This one is unique because I can choose to go on any weekend until they leave. Buying a ticket online is for a specific weekend, and there are no refunds or date changes.

Every time I look at the ticket tucked away inside the drawer in my room, it reminds me of him. The man who gifted me what I wanted, only to terrify me when I finally received it.

Since last week, all I have thought about is if I should go or when I *should* go. My mind plays different scenarios, like a first date, imagining how it would go or what you would say. What you would wear.

What if he tricks me into a dark room at one of the haunted houses? I swear I can still feel the burn of his touch on my skin since that night. That's all I could think about when I got home and have thought about every day since. After Alice dropped me off, I stared at myself in front of my bathroom mirror naked after a shower. My skin flushed from the hot water. My nipples hard with need. The ache between my thighs. I closed my eyes in front of the bathroom mirror, imagining him touching me with every stroke of my fingers until I came. My eyes opened when I felt the first wave of pleasure, memorizing the way I looked. The way my mouth parted, and my expression when my pussy clenched my fingers, wishing it was his cock. It was all I could think about since that night in the dark room of the haunted house.

Like right now, it's the same expression I see in the mirror's reflection. After I come, I bring my fingers to my mouth and suck. My cum tastes sweet, and I wonder what his tastes like. I place my fingers between my thighs, slide three fingers in my cunt and rub my clit with my thumb, fucking myself again.

PRESSING the button on the scale and place the bananas to charge a customer, I hear a familiar voice. "Hey, Ivy."I see Dean place a couple of TV dinners on the black belt behind the yellow plastic grocery store separator bar.

"Hello," I say dryly.

He is the last person I want to see. When I scan the last item, the older gentleman swipes his card, the machine spits out the receipt, and I hand it off.

After I bag the last of the gentleman's groceries, the belt runs forward. "How are you?"he asks as I scan the first TV dinner.

Beep… Beep.

"Are you okay?"he asks again.

"Yep," I quip.

I turn and bag up his food so he can be on his way. I have fifteen minutes left of my shift and want to make it home before dark.

I ring him up. There is an awkward silence while I wait for him to use the pin pad.

The machine accepts his card.

The receipt slides out.

"D-do you need a ride?" he asks with a hopeful expression.

I hand him the receipt. "No, thanks."

I watch him frown in dismay, taking the receipt. "I ended it with Sarah."

He thought he would come in here, and we would pick up where he left off? I won't come up with the money to make rent this month. My mother will go on a rant, but I'm not fucking Dean for it. Not anymore.

I cross my arms over my chest. "I'm sorry to hear that, Dean. You have a nice evening."

He grabs the bags harder than necessary, almost tearing the plastic handles off.

When he's about to walk out of the exit, he turns back around. "You should reconsider. It is dangerous out there. Did you hear about the teenage girl missing one town over?"

I've heard. Christina Marsh was reported missing when she did not return home after school. I saw the picture posted on the news alert online. She's a senior, eighteen, with strawberry-blond hair. Popular girl. Straight-A student in charge of the school newspaper with a bright future. Her mother said she wanted to be a veterinarian. She was last seen leaving school on her way home around four o'clock on September 12th. That was three days ago.

According to the news, every month, another teenage girl goes missing. The news has spread like wildfire, but no one has found out who's behind it. Rumors are there is a suspected serial killer and a bunch of theories. They make theories when they don't have facts. The authorities come up with the what-ifs, but there is no solution to stop it from happening again.

"I have."

"I can give you a ride home."

He wants to give me more than a ride, and I'm not interested. Even if he would tell me it was just for a ride, I wouldn't do it. Accepting a ride from him will give him hope. He will come back and ask again, hoping one day I'll give in.

"I told you, I don't need a ride, Dean."

I see him tense. He has a white-knuckle grip on the plastic bag. His eyes go vacant for a split second, then a shadowy grin crosses his face. "I'll keep asking, every day…until you say yes."

Pathetic.

"And I'll say no. Every day… until you stop."

"I'll never stop, Ivy."

I roll my eyes and suck my teeth. "You never fucking began, Dean."

His eyes harden when I point out what he is trying to hide. What excuse did he give Sarah? Most likely the one where he says he's stressed when he snaps.

I'm relieved when a customer pushes a grocery cart in my lane. I turn around and smile at the middle-aged woman.

"Did you find everything you were looking for today?"

"Yes, I did," she replies.

I hear the automatic doors open.

When I turn, they're sliding closed, and he's gone.

After I clear the register and clock out, I walk across the parking lot to catch the shuttle. It's still light out. The sun casts a soft golden glow across the landscape. The sky above transitions from a brilliant blue to shades of orange, pink, and purple as the sun sets. Not wanting to be caught walking home along the main highway, I hurry to the bus stop and sit on the warm bench.

I can't stop thinking of Dean's reaction when I turned him down, or what he said before he left, or the feral intensity in his eyes. I don't think he ever thought I would turn him down, but I did, and I'm proud of myself. It felt like I could finally breathe above water after removing the brick slowly weighing me down.

When the shuttle bus arrives, I hop on and walk toward the back. One man has his head leaning on the window with his eyes closed and headphones on. Another woman with fire-engine-red hair sits across from him, busy looking at her phone.

The sun has almost set when the bus drops everyone off in front of the mall. I walk inside, feel the cold air from the AC system hit my skin. Mall shoppers stop to look at the window fronts. Some walk out after they make their purchase, and some head out the front exit.

When I push the exit door to leave out the back, it's already dark. A chill slithers over my skin when a sense of unease washes over me after I round the corner.

I freeze.

In the dimly lit parking lot is a stark silhouette against the backdrop of the asphalt. It rises, casting a long and slender shadow that stretches out like a solitary sentinel.

I run back to go inside and tug on the door handle, but it doesn't budge. My hands shake.

Dread sinks in.

The door locks when you exit and can't be opened from the outside.

I look over my shoulder, and it's gone. I wipe my eyes to make sure I'm not seeing shit. Nothing. The lot is empty. I look left and right, but there is no one. I can see cars in the distance heading toward the front exit of the parking lot. There is not a single vehicle on this side.

The glow of the lights from the drive-in theater to the far right gives me a clear view of the apartment building. The light pole flickering by the general waste bin grabs my attention.

A yellow light reflects off the back of the complex by the stairwell, and I run. My bag shuffles behind me with the weight of my books. My lungs burn with the effort. The voice inside my head tells me, *Keep running. Don't stop.*

CHAPTER ELEVEN

I'M startled awake by a constant ringing. I reach for my phone but can't shut off the sound.

It's another Amber alert.

Another girl went missing. Brooke Jensen. I search for her name, and she's a junior from Fenmore High School. It's located one town over and is the same school Christina Marsh attends.

News alert says Brooke Jensen was last seen walking to her car after cheerleading practice and never made it home. No one has seen her since yesterday. Her car was towed from the parking lot at school this morning. There are no witnesses. The alert notification reads if you see something, you should say something.

I snort. "It's too late after they snatch your ass," I say aloud.

When I head out to the school bus after locking my front door, unease sets in when I see what is written on the walls by the stairwell. THEY ARE WATCHING. The next one beside it isn't any better. TO FUCK YOU.

Everyone is trying to fuck someone, I tell myself.

After last night, I have been trying to piece together what I saw or thought I saw. Was the man standing in the parking lot real? Is it because I'm paranoid?

Every month, they find another body of a missing girl, but they haven't found the person responsible.

I have to remain vigilant and keep in mind there is a killer or killers out there. One thing those girls have in common when they come up missing is that they were all alone when it happened. It means I can't walk home, or I could be their next target. My thought flies to Dean and his incessant behavior about taking me home.

WHEN THE BELL RINGS, I shut my locker and turn the lock. It's my last class, but I need to use the restroom. I don't care about science. I already did all the work and turned it in. I'm about to make a quick left to the women's bathroom when I see Jason walking with one of his teammates Paul Carson. Paul gives me a once-over. Jason murmurs something to Paul, but from where he's standing, I can't make out what he says.

Jason walks closer. "Hey, Ivy," he says, gripping his crotch. "Are you ready for this big cock?"

Paul smirks, but it quickly fades when I shoot back with, "Looks like Paul is getting you off nicely. As soon as you grabbed your junk, his face lit up."

Jason's eyes narrow, and his jaw hardens. "Are you calling me a faggot?"

"I think the correct term is gay, and there is nothing wrong with it. You two look good together. I think it's cute he walks you to class"—I smile—"whispering to each other."

"Come here, and I'll show you how gay I am. Paul can watch."

Fear claws my gut because I know he would show me, and it doesn't involve Paul participating. The look in his eyes is feral.

The hallway is empty. The silence begins to stretch with every second. His mouth widens with a malevolent smile. He charges forward, and I bolt inside the women's restroom.

I run inside the last stall, sliding the lock shut and hearing the groan of the bathroom close. My chest is rising and falling. A scream is lodged in my throat.

My ears strain to hear the groan of the bathroom door, looking through the tiny crack in the stall door. Hoping they didn't follow me. All I hear is the sound of my rapid breathing, and I feel the burn in my lungs.

I hear footsteps outside.

"Oh God," I whisper.

I step back, hoping it's a girl who needs to pee. I take another step back and feel something hard behind me. When I turn, my scream is muffled when a large hand covers my mouth and a body pins me against the stall.

It's him.

"Shh…."

My eyes widen, taking in the white-and-black face paint like a jester. He is wearing a black hooded sweater.

I'm trying to make out his face, but all I can make out are his full lips, a sharp jaw, and a straight nose. What has me mesmerized is how dark his eyes are. They are dark, like a bottomless pool of ink holding secrets in their depths.

I try to move, but he shakes his head. The door

groans when it opens, and a sense of overwhelming terror washes over me like a suffocating tide.

"We know you're in here, Ivy. We just want to talk to you for a minute. I need to handle this thing we have between us." *Slam!* They begin pushing each door with a force that rattles the stalls. "I promised to show you what you're missing." *Slam!* The next stall door opens with force.

My eyes refocus on the man in front of me with his head canted to the side. How did he get in here? How did he know?

They know I'm in here, but don't know he's here with me. He raises his finger over my lips, and I notice the ink on his hands, but I can't determine what they are. He pushes me slowly behind him and motions for me to sit on the toilet.

Another door slams open. "I know you're here, Ivy. Don't be shy. I just want to show you, baby. I promise I can fuck you harder than Tommy."

My masked performer's cavernous eyes flick down to mine. A thunderous drumbeat pulses in my ears. The tension builds like a bomb ready to go off. He rolls his neck like he's getting ready to do something strenuous.

He gives me his back, and I let out a shallow breath.

Everything goes quiet.

I hear the lock open with a click.

"That's it, baby. Come out," Jason coos.

"We want to play, Ivy," Paul says darkly. "We want to hear you scream like you did for Tommy."

Oh my God. They want to rape me.

My masked hero pushes the door open. My chest tightens when the door swings back.

"What the fuck?" Paul and Jason say in tandem.

Then a cacophony of noises. The sound of violence being unleashed—skin meeting flesh in rapid succession. A loud thud followed by groans, and metal. The ground trembles when flesh and bone hits the floor.

I stand on the toilet and hunch over. My gut is churning. I try to see what is happening through the open door, but then I hear a loud crunch and then…nothing.

After a few seconds, I hear footsteps.

The bathroom door squeaks.

I hold my breath, slide one foot and the other from the toilet seat. I lean to look between the crack from the stall door. Paul and Jason are out cold on the bathroom floor. Paul's arm lies at an awkward angle. My masked hero is gone.

"WHAT HAPPENED?" PRINCIPAL Miller asks.

"I told you. I didn't see anything. I was in the stall and heard the bathroom door open. There was a scuffle—"

"You didn't come out to see what was going on?"

"I was using the toilet. I wasn't going to walk out with my pants down—"

"You expect me to believe that, Ivy."

Principal Miller has been working at this school for the past twenty-five years. He is bald at the top of his head with hair on the sides like he refuses to cut off the rest so it's even. He has a round belly as if he just swallowed a whole watermelon because the rest of him is skinny. His throat is irritated with bumps from shaving.

He drives an old station wagon and likes to drill students he thinks are trouble. Basically, the ones who don't play sports or have parents with deep pockets. I don't fit any of his requirements except the one that requires a private room and his right hand. He thinks I didn't notice him adjusting his brown slacks when the lady at the front desk showed me in. He wears flannels every day to school and golf pants. Who the fuck wears flannels with golf pants? And don't get me started on his glasses. He looks like he kills fire ants in his spare time with how thick they are.

I slouch in the chair and look at the picture of his family on his desk. Two girls, and they look bored just like his wife. All three brunettes. The frame reminds me of the ones you find at the dollar store. Nothing I say is good enough. He wants someone to blame because his precious football team is out of two of their starting play-ers. How is that my fault?

"It's not my fault they chose the bathroom to fight whoever it was, and I was in the stall taking a piss, if you must know."

"That's enough, young lady. I don't know if your mother allows you to be disrespectful, but I won't tolerate it."

"It's hard when you're trying to blame me for some-thing I didn't do. There is no way it was me."

"You're covering up for someone, and I don't know why."

"I didn't see anything, so how is that possible?"

He looks at me steadily. "You're suspended for two weeks."

I sit up. "What? Why? I didn't do it. You're acting like I did."

"Two students on the starting football team are out for the season because they were beaten up in the girl's bathroom during school. And...you were there and didn't do anything. You also happened not to see anything either. Which means... you are hiding who did it."

I overheard him on the phone talking to their parents. Paul has a broken arm, and Jason has a few cuts and bruises on his face and body. His ankle and hand are questionable. The doctors said they couldn't play the rest of the season if they planned on making it to college.

I scoff. "Are you hearing yourself right now? What was I supposed to do? Go after whoever did it? Fight? This is stupid. Whatever happened has nothing to do with me. You haven't asked if anything happened to me."

He blinks like a reptile. "That's it…" He walks over to the door and opens it with more force than necessary. "Out!" he shouts. "Come back to school two Mondays from now. I'll inform your teachers, and I suggest you pick up any work you need to turn in while you are suspended. You wouldn't want to repeat your senior year a third time, Miss Sloan."

What an asshole.

"Whatever."

I stand, and right before I leave, he says, "The police will be in touch if they require anything. It would behoove you, Miss Sloan, to cooperate. Your senior year is on the line."

I smile sarcastically. "I hope you catch whoever did it

because we both know it wasn't me. And"—I point at the bulge in his crotch—" you should take care of that, or you might not make it to retirement, Mr. Miller." His face turns red.

I hope they don't catch him because those two idiots deserved to get their asses kicked. It would be pointless to tell Mr. Miller the truth because he wouldn't believe me anyway. Even if he did, I wouldn't say shit.

"Be careful what you say, Miss Sloan…your reputation around school isn't the best."

I shake my head. Unbelievable.

"Your reputation to find the truth isn't either, Mr. Miller," I shot back and walk out and continue, "Thank you for the chat. I'm sure you will have the report of our conversation sent to the counselor." I turn around, I look at the huge bulge in his pants and smile. "Don't leave anything out." And walk out.

He shuts the door with a slam.

On the positive side, I could pick up shifts at the Big H and earn money I need for the rent. I could also pay my masked hero a visit at the circus to thank him.

CHAPTER TWELVE

"HERE." I hand my mother one hundred and fifty dollars.

She looks up after taking a drag from her morning cigarette, takes the money, and stuffs it in her bra.

"Why aren't you at school?" she asks after blowing smoke from her lips. "Took my advice and dropped out."

"No. I got suspended."

She chuckles and takes another drag. Her upper lip wrinkles, reminding me of beef jerky when she sucks on her cancer stick. I try to hold my breath when she does it. It will take me twenty-five minutes to air out the apartment followed by another shower.

"What did you do?"

"Nothing. I was in the bathroom when two guys came in fighting, and the principal suspended me because I didn't know who kicked their ass. I was in the bathroom stall taking a piss."

This is the version I'm going with, not like my mother cares. Her focus is on me coming up with the rent money, and her advice is to use my body to get it.

"What does that have to do with you?"

"Exactly. It's none of my business who fights and who gets beat up. I didn't see anything, and I'm no snitch."

"How long?"

"Two weeks."

"You got the other half of the rent?"

"I got the light."

She snuffs out the cigarette in her coffee. "I didn't ask you that, Ivy. I asked if you have the other half of the rent. The diner is slow, and I'm not making enough in tips."

Not for cigarettes. She smokes a pack a day. There is always enough for those.

"I'll ask for more hours during my suspension. It's all I can do."

"Well…if you don't, you will have to find somewhere else to live."

"But Mom—"

"I'm sick and tired of telling you, Ivy. I've told you to quit school—"

"If I finish, I can get a better job."

"We moved because you threw a fit about Hank, and I told you what you had to do. You think you're better than me. That you are going to make a ton of money. The only job you'll get is spreading your legs, and you might as well get a head start. You won't be young forever, which is why Hank wanted you. If you would have agreed, we wouldn't have had to move here."

I flinch. Hank shoved his cock in my throat and forced me to do other things I didn't want. My mother didn't care that he did. She cared more about her not being pretty enough to keep his attention. Hank is a meth dealer. He paid attention to my mother because he wanted to take advantage of me, and she hates me for it.

She knows I would never have agreed to do it. This is her way to blame me.

"Why are you like this?"

She gets up and digs in her front uniform pocket for another cigarette. "Because it's how we pay rent. It's how we eat. It is reality." She lights the cigarette until the tip glows red. "Come up with the money or get out, Ivy. Either way, you will be under someone. Hank, the married asshole from the Big H, another asshole that doesn't like his wife's cunt because she's a nag"—she takes a drag—"he will do anything for a young cunt."

"Like rape and kill them. Haven't you seen the news?"

"I have, and you know what, those are the dumb ones who get snatched up unawares. Because they think men aren't monsters. Those little pricks at your school think with their dicks at a young age, and it doesn't get better as they get older. Don't think for one second there is a special prince who will come save you on his white horse. The white horse is a van to take advantage of you, and when they're done, they get rid of you. That's the truth. It's sad for those girls." She nods like she needs to convince herself of the bullshit she's spewing. She takes a drag, then another, and continues, "If they had a mother or a parent to tell them the way of the world, they would be better prepared. I'm doing you a favor, Ivy. I'm telling you what men see when they look at you. A short skirt, pretty face, and pair of tits. Use it to your advantage while you can. You'll thank me later."And with that, she grabs her keys and walks out the door.

I wish I could yell at her and tell her she's lying. I wish I could tell her she is bitter because she didn't do more with her life and blames me. But the truth is I can't because everything she said about men is true. Not the girls—it's not their fault. It's not their fault vile people exist.

But guys like Dean, guys at school, Kevin at the Big H, Hank, and Scott, the drug dealer. They all prove my mother right. Only one so far has proved her wrong. The one who saved me. The one I don't know but know where to find. The man who stopped the minute I said no. The man I can't stop thinking about and need to see.

I SHOVE my small duffel inside my employee locker and shut the door.

"You said you needed to see me?" Kevin says from the doorway.

I grab my name tag and walk out of the employee's lounge.

"I wanted to ask if I could pick up any full-time shifts this week and next week."

He smirks. "Dropping out of school?"

"No. I have some time off. Can you give me the shifts or not?"

I'm not going to beg him. He can kiss my ass.

His eyes land on my chest. "I can work something out."

"I also need to leave in time to catch the last shuttle after every shift from now on."

"I can't make any promises about that."

"Haven't you heard the news?"

"I have, but I don't see what that has to do with you receiving special treatment. Hanna doesn't. Trisha doesn't."

Hanna is sixty-three and has a husband who picks her up. Trisha is twenty-eight, pimpled-faced, weighs about three hundred pounds, and blames it on having four kids. She lives with her grandmother and drives a minivan. I'm not judging, but neither of them is a teenager going to high school. The girls that have been found dead are all juniors and seniors in high school. Trisha and Hanna both have a way to get home, but I don't tell him that.

"I don't want to walk home after the sun sets."

"What happened to your ride?"

He means Dean. I'm sure he thinks the worst, and he's right.

"He has a girlfriend."

"Oh." His eyes lift. "I could give you a ride," he offers. "It's no trouble."

"That's okay. I'm fine taking the shuttle."

"I can't make any promises, Ivy. I can't let you leave early every day. It's not fair to the other employees, but I can give you a ride home," he offers.

I don't miss the intent behind it or the way his eyes undress me as he says it.

"Don't worry about it. I'll try to make it work."

"Offer still stands, Ivy. I don't mind."

I'm sure you don't.

"Do you need me at register five today, Kevin," Trisha asks, looking between me and Kevin.

Trisha is nice but is overwhelmed by being a single

mom. You can tell she had a rough night with the bags under her eyes. She works hard, but Kevin treats her like shit.

"No. I need you to stock the shelves."

"Why can't Ricky do it?" I ask.

"Because I said so, Ivy. Now get to your lane."

Stocking shelves sucks, and he makes her do it all the time.

"I'll switch with her," I offer.

Trisha looks relieved. I bet her back and feet are killing her. I stocked shelves my first day working here, and my feet killed me for two days straight. My back felt like it was trampled on.

"Are you the manager of this store now, Ivy? "

"No, Kevin. I'm not, but I've stocked shelves, and it's a lot of work when you do it every day. It also helps to work in other areas in the store in case someone calls out."

Trisha smiles at me like I'm her savior. I'm not, but someone needs to help her out. Her feet look like they got stung by bees. They are red and puffy, and the flats she is wearing are warped.

"Is that what you want, Ivy?" he asks, making my skin crawl.

"We could rotate. She can handle the register, and I'll stock in the morning, and then we can switch in the afternoon."

"Fine," he agrees, "if you need a ride after, let me know."

When he walks away, I swallow the nausea pricking my throat.

Trisha passes by me and says softly, "Thanks, Ivy. He can be a prick sometimes."

"More like all the time," I tell her, watching him walk into the management office.

"If you need a ride today, I can take you. My mom can watch the kids for ten more minutes."

A thought crosses my mind.

"I normally wouldn't say yes, knowing you need to get home to your babies after working all day, but could you drop me off at the fair?"

"The fair?"

I smile. "Yeah."

CHAPTER THIRTEEN

AFTER TRISHA DROPS ME OFF, I walk to the closest booth at the entrance of the haunted Carnival. I hand the man dressed in a clown costume my ticket.

He takes it, shines a light on it, and looks up. "Hold out your left hand, please." He fastens a red band around my left wrist. "That's a special band, do not take it off." He secures a black band. "This band is for unlimited rides. The red is for the VIP area at the Circle of Freaks Show. They will scan your ID at the entrance to verify your age. Then leave your bag and phone with security."

My heart pounds in excitement.

"Thank you."

He hands me my special ticket for tonight's show at the Circle of Freaks tent and a carnival map. "Thank you for coming. We've been DYING to have you," he says in a deep, slow cadence.

I walk in and head through the fog. It's different from the first time. A bit scarier because I'm alone. There is no one I can hold on to if I'm scared.

My heart beats so fast I can feel my blood pumping in my ears like a drum. The fog around me is thick. A couple walks ahead of me through the mist and disappear. I look to my left and right, waiting for something to appear. But nothing. I pass the signs that read, ABANDON ALL HOPE, KILLING BOOTH, and I CAN SMELL YOUR FEARS.

The couple walking ahead scream. The fog clears. The actor with the bloody mask glances at me and walks away. Why didn't he scare me? I look down at my wrist. Is it the band? Are they not allowed to frighten me because of it?

I spot a palm concession booth.

A woman walks out, planting herself in front of me, and asks, "Would you like a reading?"

She has a British accent. It sounds nice. Different from the Southern twang I learned to hide when we moved here. I always pictured a fortune teller as having a Romany accent when in character. She wears a long, gauzy skirt, big hoop earrings, and a shawl with different occult symbols. Her hair was black with gray streaks beginning from her temples.

"I'm not sure?" I tell her.

I'm curious but don't want to seem eager. I know whatever she is going to say is a lie, but it looks fun.

"You doubt me," she announces. "I assure you, I'm not."

"Oh, I…"

She grabs my hand and looks at my palm. "Come with me." She looks up. "I won't charge you."

"Why not?'

"You're special." She leans close. "He would be so disappointed in me if I did."

I pinch my brows in confusion. "Who?"

"Come," she says and pulls me to her booth. "I don't have much time before the show starts, and he's waiting."

How did she… and then I look at my wrist. It's no secret she is talking about the show. I'm wearing the band. Anyone could have guessed where I was headed. But what did she mean when she said *he*?

"Who is…? "

She tugs me inside. "Have a seat," she says.

She sits on the opposite side of the table, covered with a dark purple cloth adorned with golden motifs that shimmer subtly under the low light of flickering candles. A medium-sized crystal ball rests on the table, emitting a shimmering radiance from its surface. Scattered throughout are many old items, such as polished stones, tarnished coins, and intricate metal charms, each carrying a mysterious and magical aura.

Her chair has luxurious velvet upholstery and a finely embroidered tapestry portraying whirling galaxies and magical sigils hanging on the wall, contrasting the horror theme outside.

She holds out her hand, motioning for mine. She takes my hand and leans close, closing her eyes and moving her lips in a silent prayer.

When she's done, she opens her eyes and begins, "You are his chosen one. The one he has been waiting for."

"Chosen one?"

"Shh…I'm not finished. I will give you a reading. Believe me or not. You can do with it as you wish."

"Okay, my name is Ivy. What is your name?"

"Madam Seraphina," she says and continues, "You were chosen since before your time. Fate has brought you here, and you have a gift." Her eyes stare at me intently. "You draw people. Men of the opposite sex are entranced. Women mesmerized. This is your power, but it's to be shown and only given to one. You were his, and he was yours before you took your first breath." She traces the line on the palm of my hand, tickling my skin. "The house chose you. It holds secrets. Secrets that continue the circle of life for generations. Anyone who tries to break the circle dies." She looks up. "You will have a family and bear another son. One woman in their lineage bears two sons, and one day, you will have a vision of the future to pass down to your son. Don't doubt your dreams, Ivy. All your wishes will come true, but with the good, you need to accept the bad. Bad people exist, and some must die. It is all that I'm allowed to tell you. It will all make sense."

"Who's he?"

I ask, not believing a word she's saying. A house. A family. All my dreams coming true. It's fun and nice to hear. Also, very generic. How many people does she spin this bizarre tale to? But nonetheless, I'm curious.

She releases my hand and caresses the crystal ball. "He will be the one who makes you feel what no other has made you feel. He is…everything in your world. He will scare you. He will make you scream in rapture. *He* will do anything for you. You are the air he needs to breathe. You will know who *he* is because he will captivate you the same way you captivate him."

AFTER THE FUN reading with Madam Seraphina, I make it to the entrance of the Circus of Freaks—the red-and-white tent with lights shooting up toward the sky. Red lights run parallel on each side. I noticed four tents connected in the back and two late-model luxury RVs. It's amazing. You feel the excitement before you step inside.

There is a red carpet and a man with a scanner wearing a black cloth mask covering his entire head. He swipes an ID and looks up to check if it matches the same person before waving them through the metal detectors. Three more men in suits with similar masks take cell phones and bags, placing them in bins. He hands each person a ticket to claim their belongings.

I give the man my ID. He scans it and hesitates before handing it to a man behind him.

"Is there a problem?" I ask, but they both ignore me.

The second man scans my ID on a reader and returns it.

"Go ahead," he says, gesturing me forward.

"Is everything alright?"

He turns to the next person, dismissing me.

Dick.

I turn in my phone and small duffel bag before passing through the metal detectors. When the curtain pulls up to let me through, I stop. The tent is dimly lit. I expected bleachers and heat. The smell of plastic, like the tents schools set up for outdoor events.

Instead, I find air blowers. Comfortable seating. Rich decor. It looks like the interior of a Las Vegas hotel I've seen on TV, but what has me fascinated is the stage.

There is a catwalk with lights coming out of a huge mouth of a clown with red lights for the eyes.

To my right and left are pictures of clowns painted on canvas resting on easels. Grotesque creatures and performers. A sign to my right says:

ENTER IF YOU DARE TO GET FUCKED

To my left it reads:

THE WICKED SUFFER HERE.

Only five people are seated at the front closest to the stage, sanctioned off with a sign that says: RESERVED RED BANDS ONLY.

I look at my wrist, impressed at the choice of seating. Women walk down the aisles with trays of food and drinks, wearing top hats, corsets, short skirts, and fishnets.

I have ten minutes before the show, so I turn left to see the exhibits.

I walk deeper into a makeshift hallway with props of headless men on gurneys with bloody sheets. There are pickle jars sealed with what looks like fake body parts. Eyes, fingers, and…cocks on a display shelf.

It smells like the fog machines outside mixed with a weird scent. It smells like the lab at school when I dissected a frog in middle school. The teacher said it was formaldehyde, a fluid used to preserve tissue. My stomach turns when I see eyeballs staring back at me.

I walk deeper and see a body whose head has no eyes, and his fingers and cock were cut off. He's tied like Jesus on a cross with rope on his wrists and ankles. A wooden stake is in the ground behind him, holding his torso and neck.

I get close, curiosity eating me. It's fake. It has to be.

There is no way they can have real bodies tied up like this for a circus show. The skin has a sheen from the red light above. It looks like a man. There is no blood and looks embalmed. The center of his torso has been sewn with a thick string like the insides were scraped out.

I've never seen a dead body up close before, but this looks as close as you can get without killing someone. I'm dying to see what the performers look like.

Heading back, I watch as people begin to take their seats. The tent is full. People you would never guess who would like the circus. Couples of all ages. Old, young, and middle-aged ready to watch the show.

Metal gates lead to the center aisle. A flashing red sign says the BUTCHER. A man walks out, and it's disturbing. He's shirtless with two pieces of human leg props with blood dripping in each hand. His face is painted white. Eyes red. He licks one of the legs. His teeth glow. Blood drops out of his mouth.

Security lets me through after I show my band, and I sit on a black leather seat.

The light dims. The red light shines bright from the open mouth in the center of the stage.

The tent grows quiet.

The audience waits anxiously for the show to begin. Music starts as clowns run out of the mouth onto the stage. They move through the audience with mischievous energy. People laugh nervously between humor and horror. The clowns turn their heads in awkward angles, waving knives in the air. One throws one up and catches it with his mouth before hitting a woman.

My lips lift in a smile, feeling the excitement and adrenaline in the room.

An illusionist takes the stage. Eliciting awes from the crowd and then a scream when a clown startles another with a knife.

The music shifts to "Kore" by DEADON-CAROUSEL.

Knives from the clowns levitate. The illusionist gestures toward them with his hands floating through the air. The Butcher interferes. Drops the leg and grabs the knife, slicing the leg repeatedly. He removes his shirt. Fire shoots out behind him, and the Butcher levitates his body, ripped with muscle.

A tube with smoke is shoved in front of me. I look to my left. It's the woman from the roller coaster.

She licks her lips with a smile like we share a secret. "Here. Drink it."

I look at the tube. It seems like a shot of something.

"I don't have any money."

She leans close. Her face was painted ghostly white. Her lips blood red. She smells like something fruity I want to lick.

"I don't want your money. I want you to drink." Her lips ghost my ear. "He wouldn't want you to be thirsty."

I turn so that our lips are almost touching. "Who?"

Her eyes fall to my lips. "Be careful, I like pussy."

"Well…I don't lick."

"Good. He prefers sucking."

"Who are you talking about?" I ask.

She's beautiful. Her makeup is flawless. Her eyes are lined with thick black eyeliner and red eye shadow.

"You'll see." Her eyes drop to the tube she's holding between us. "Drink. I want to see you swallow." I take it from her hands and wrap my lips around the top. The swell of her breasts lift as she watches me tilt my head back and drink. It's fruity and burns down my throat. I hand her the empty tube. She angles her head robotically. "Was it good, Ivy?"

I furrow my brows. "How—"

She takes the tube and walks away, swaying her hips.

How did she know my name?

Darkness blankets the tent, and the music stops. People cheer and scream in the dark. Electronic music begins to play a haunting beat. The stage is empty. Fire shoots out. Heat fills the air for a beat.

A man in a top hat appears dressed in an impeccably tailored coat. The music shifts to "The Clock Strikes Midnight" by Icky Ichabod. Bells go off in a haunting melody as the man reveals himself.

His coat is a rich burgundy, catching a glint of the red spotlight. The coat flows gracefully over his ripped, muscled frame. He has tattoos all over his chest and stomach. Intricate designs dipped in his muscles over his skin. The man is pure strength with an athletic physique. When he walks upstage, his high collar gives off Victorian elegance.

His face is painted white like a skull—black around his eyes, nose, and lips.

"Welcome to the Circle of Freaks. My name is Draco, and…" He pauses. My eyes lift, mesmerized. It's him. There's no mistake. It's my masked hero. His eyes land on mine, and he announces, "I'm the ringmaster."

My hands are sweating. My stomach does a little flip. He's gorgeous. Chiseled jaw, dark eyes, straight nose, and cheekbones so defined it would make a *Vogue* model jealous.

His top hat tilts to the side. His piercing eyes command the stage. It's like he holds the power of everyone's attention in his hands.

The audience claps and cheers.

"First, we bring you the wicked. The ones who don't deserve to live among you. If you feel that you will not be able to handle the show…please leave. Now is the time. Once the gate closes…you belong to the Circle of Freaks," he warns in a deep tone.

Everyone looks around, and a few get up and leave. He waits until they are gone, then the gate locks. Three security guards with suits and black masks stand in front.

"Now," Draco's voice echoes. "We can begin." The Butcher and another man with grotesque makeup push three men tied to chairs with wheels. They have a gag in each of their mouths. "Here we are," Draco says with a menacing smile. "I've been waiting for you."

You could hear the muffled screams from the men. The red lights glow over the three of their faces. Their eyes bulging out of their sockets. *It's fake. They're actors.*

"Ringmaster's Show" by DEADONTHECAROSEL blares from the speakers. Three women walk up behind the men and pull their hair back roughly like they're drinking blood.

The knives from the illusionists fly in the air, gesturing

with his hands. The knives land, slicing their necks. Blood squirts, and the knives drop.

"Oh…" one guy says behind me.

"It looks real," his girlfriend says.

"It isn't," he replies.

I'm sitting on the edge of my seat because I'm not so sure. It does look real. Like the three men are being murdered. The air is tinged with a metallic smell.

The three women levitate from the suspension wire. They twirl in the air, defying the laws of gravity by their long hair.

I recognize one of them being the one from the roller coaster as she lands on her feet. A wicked laugh bubbles from her throat. She swipes her hands over her white hair. Her neck tilts back, and she's suspended by her hair, this time floating above the audience.

My hand flies over my mouth. Her neck could snap, but it doesn't. She's in total control. She's spectacular. A true talent.

When she lands safely, the crowd goes wild. Draco looks up, and jealousy grips me from the admiration in his gaze. I would do anything to have a man look at me like that.

CHAPTER FOURTEEN

WHEN THE SHOW IS OVER, I turn right to the area I didn't get to explore. It's blocked off about three feet inside. The show was everything—the ringmaster was everything. If I had paid, it would have been worth every penny.

I'm about to walk back out when security blocks my path. He motions for my band.

"Oh…I only have a black and red one. I'm sorry, I didn't know I wasn't allowed here."

He points behind me. I look over, and his partner gestures for me to go in. It would have been simpler to tell me that part, but not speaking is part of the show.

I'm let through, and the atmosphere changes. It smells sweet. It feels colder than the main stage. I look behind me, but security doesn't follow. The lighting glows red. I'm in one of the back tents I saw from the outside. Metal skeletons line the walls like soldiers in a palace.

The area opens to a stage in the center. It's much smaller than the main one, but this stage has mirrors on the floor. A throne in the center like it's waiting for its king. There is a walkway that leads to a glass enclosure. The glass is a bit fogged, but as I get closer, I notice props and chains on a St. Andrews cross and…sex furniture.

I know what they are called because I researched it when I was watching porn and wanted to know what the special chairs and beds were used for.

To the left of the room, there is a red and black sex chair. In the center is a bondage table and a fun stool to the right. I look up, and it's completely enclosed and can only be accessed from the back. Is this where they...

A man in a leather mask walks inside, and my breath catches in my throat. He's wearing a hooded cloak and black leather pants. He pushes the cloak over each shoulder. His body is chiseled. He is ripped with muscle and tattoos. He's perfect.

A woman walks in, and I recognize her from the show, dressed in a corset with no bra. Her nipples stand proud pink and hard. Her hair is white, and I can tell she's wearing a wig. She is wearing black-and-white clown makeup. She walks in her sky-high, shiny black stilettos and bends at the waist over the bondage table. Her ass is in the air. The netted tights she is wearing are attached to a garter, giving the man a full view of her shaved pussy.

I clench my legs together when he stands behind her spreading her ass cheeks open. My clit tingles. He dips his head and licks her slit. My heart begins to beat like a jackhammer. The illusionist walks in dressed the same way without the cloak. His eyes are lined with Guyliner.

He's good-looking—they all are.

Gorgeous bodies and pretty faces.

He walks close to the glass and blows hot air, fogging up the glass. He writes KEIR.

"Keir," I say out loud. He nods. "Your name?"

He nods again.

More performers walk in. Three females and eight men dressed the same way. I even recognized the clown the night I came with Alice. His eyes sweep over me, but what has my attention since the first time I saw them is the ringmaster. He walks tall and commanding toward the woman who gave me the shot. The one he looks at like she's everything.

The familiar pang of jealousy grips me again, squeezing my throat. He approaches her and grabs her delicate neck in his big hand. She looks up at him with a salacious smile. Her red lips are glossy under the lights.

Keir turns, giving me his back. Draco doesn't notice I'm watching, and I am not sure if I'm happy or disappointed. My mind wanders to the day in the bathroom and why he was there, but that thought quickly evaporates. The first couple starts fucking. He slides his cock inside her ass after squeezing a bottle of lube over her ass and pussy. Her forehead wrinkles, followed by a moan. I can see the pure lust in her eyes when he thrusts inside her. Another man in a clown outfit shoves his cock in her mouth. She makes a choking sound as she takes him deep.

I place the palm of my hand over the glass and notice the little holes. I can hear them. The slapping of skin as the Butcher takes her hard, grunting with each thrust.

My eyes swing to Draco, but Keir never moves like he is a shield. I don't know why. I step to the side and my eyes are transfixed on Draco and the beautiful woman. Was he blocking me from seeing them?

She drops to her knees like a servant. She undoes his pants, licking her lips like he's a delicious meal she can't do without. I don't want to watch, but my feet don't cooperate because curious I want to see his cock. I've imagined him fucking me since that night in the haunted house. I remind myself that he's a man. Not some bull-shit hero I made up in my mind or some guy a fake fortune teller told me about.

He takes.

He uses.

The way my mother warned me about. This man is no prince, and I'm no one in his eyes.

In my fantasy, he was a demigod. The one who would save and want me, but it is all a lie. A stupid crush I made because my life is so shitty. For a second, he had the power. The power to make me feel like I was important somehow. But now, he's going to fuck her. He's going to pleasure her while she pleasures him. They're perfect for each other. I could never be what she is to him.

Draco's gaze falls to her pretty face. I can find no flaw in her when I'm full of them.

I'm ashamed to say I was hoping to find one in her, but there isn't. I could never compete. I could never belong to someone like him.

I'm used.

I'm a woman who sold her pussy for a hundred bucks at a time, taking up the oldest profession in the world. I'm nothing like these people. They're talented. They respect each other and are free to be whoever they want. Gorgeous people who hold their own power.

I'm trapped, damaged, and talentless.

Draco frees his cock, and she licks her lips. Keir stiffens.

He turns to face me, but I'm already turning to walk away. I've seen enough. I know what happens next. They role-play. BDSM. She is his pet. His submissive. It's part of their show and makes sense. It will attract a crowd without the public participating. It's genius. A show after the main show. Who knows what other stuff they are into?

When I walk out, three couples walk inside.

Enjoy the show.

The Circle of Freaks are well…freaks.

When I leave the tent, I walk through the park, glad more people are walking around enjoying the food and rides.

My stomach growls.

I stop at a food stand that sells a tub with a kabob of meat that resembles guts. If I weren't so hungry, I would pass, but the smell has me salivating. It smells like barbecued steak. There is a glaze over the chunk of meat that looks delicious.

I pay for my food and grab the same drink from the guy wearing the jester costume. I place the five bucks on his cart this time and grab a bloody drink.

I ignore him when he calls out, "Hey! Take that back."

I find a spot at a table away from everyone. I was replaying my experience at the circus. It was the best performance I have ever seen in my life. I have to admit the last part I wish I was part of. The sex looked fun. The women were enjoying it. The look on their faces was a reward for the men who gave them pleasure.

Pleasure exists when it's with the right person. I admit I have bad luck. I've never experienced pleasure in a man's hands. Maybe I'm doomed. Cursed. I don't captivate a man or mesmerize a woman. Such bullshit.

"Are you always alone?" I look up. Keir.

I swallow and wipe my mouth with a napkin. "How did you find me?"

He sits, noting he isn't wearing leather pants but black jeans, boots, and a black T-shirt. He has a wallet chain that clanks against the bench when he stretches his long legs.

"Security notified me where you went. Why did you leave?"

I look around, noting that he isn't with his friends. "I saw enough. It's not fun when you're not participating."

His brows shoot up when he turns to face me. "Is that why you left?"

I couldn't stomach the man I fantasized about being pleasured by another woman.

I knew that it wasn't jealousy I felt. It was envy.

I take a sip of the red soda. His gaze falls to my lips. They must be stained red. The last time I drank this, I had to brush my teeth twice when I got home.

"I was interested in the circus— the main show," I point out. "I saw what I wanted."

"Did you like the show?"

I grin. "I loved it."

"I'm Keir."

"I know. You wrote it on the glass. My name is ... Ivy Sloan."

"I like it."

"Huh?"

"Your name. Ivy Sloan. It's nice. Strong."

"Thank you."

You should hear what they call me at school.

"What was your favorite part of the show?" he asks.

The ringmaster, but I don't tell him that. He wants to know what I thought of his performance. I can see in his eyes how important it is to him. What the audience thinks is important to any performer. I would be the same way if I had the talent to perform. I have to say it was his—the illusionist. I also liked the woman who had Draco's attention, but I thought his was the best.

"I liked yours."

"Are you saying that to be nice because I'm sitting here?"

"No. Honestly, I liked yours. The knives were spectacular. I liked all the performers—"

"How about Draco?"

I look at the bucket of meat kabobs in my hands. "He was good."

He was extraordinary, but I would never admit that. I need to forget about him, and fangirling him isn't the way to do it.

"Some say there is nothing like him. The only of his kind."

"Some...but not all."

I flinch when he reaches behind me and produces a black rose like magic. My eyes go wide when he hands it to me. I take the stem and look behind him, but there is nothing. How?

"Don't be afraid."

"I-I wasn't expecting that. I was right." I hold up the rose. "Yours was better."

"Thank you. I'm glad to hear it. It means a lot."

I check the time and decided to get a cab or Uber home. It's almost ten, and it's getting colder. I can't afford to come back to the fair. I'm pushing it as it is with the food I bought, but I have enough to get home.

I get up and toss the bucket with one hand in the trash and then do the same with the cup of red soda. "I should get going."

He looks around like he's waiting for someone to materialize. "You're leaving?"

"It's getting late. If you could thank Draco for me… for the ticket. It was my first time at a circus, and I'll never forget it. When I was a little girl, I would fantasize being part of one,"I admit and pick up my duffel bag. "Bye, Keir. It was nice meeting you."

"It was a pleasure, Ivy," he says, tilting his head, but I don't miss the tinge of a British accent he tries to hide.

When I walk away, I feel his gaze on my back.

I pass through the fog that floats like a chrome cloud of smoke toward the exit with my phone in hand, tracking the Uber driver. Four minutes.

When I look up and the fog clears, I stop.

Draco is bowing before me, wearing his coat and top hat with another ticket. The Butcher and the woman who was sucking him off flank his sides but at a distance.

I take two steps. "Thank you for the opportunity, but I can't take it."

He straightens, eyes dark, face painted like a skull looming over me. It feels like time has stood still.

"Did you not like the show?" He asks in a deep voice.

"I loved the show. You all were spectacular, and I'll never forget it." His gaze falls to the rose in my hand. "You were all so great. "And I meant it. I look between him, the Butcher, and pause on the woman I envy. "You both look great together," I tell her. Her eyes dart to

Draco wide like saucers, but his gaze holds something I'm familiar with. Fear. I can't explain why. What could he be afraid of? "Thank you for the other day," I tell him.

I wait for him to say something, but he doesn't. No, *you're welcome.* Nothing. I check my phone. My ride is waiting for me at the exit. I glance at him again, knowing I will never meet anyone like him. "It was nice meeting you, Draco."

CHAPTER FIFTEEN
DRACO

"I'M SORRY," Nyx rushes out. "I didn't know she was there, Draco."

Ignoring her apology, I stare at the empty stage, hating myself for walking in with Nyx. I admit I wanted to forget her. Like I've done since I felt her tremble underneath my fingers. That night on the roller coaster and again in the haunted house.

After the show, I thought she had left to go to the rides and needed to get a grip on the power she had over me. I didn't plan on letting it get that far with Nyx. Not now.

Keir walks in, and I swing at his face with my fist. He didn't see it coming, given the look of surprise on his face. I feel his skin split between my knuckles. I hit him again and feel his lips mash his teeth. Blood drips out of his mouth and down his chin.

"What the fuck do you think you were doing with her?"

He shakes his head, trying to shake off the two blows I landed. He staggers, but I don't give a shit. I lunge at him again, and he takes the blows. I pummel him, and he takes it.

He steps back, and I keep punching. I don't fight him like I would someone else. I can't. He doesn't know. I caught how she smiled at him seated on the bench. A smile she had never given me, and he took it.

He spits on the ground. "I was trying to get her to stay. It wasn't my fault."

"The rose wasn't your fault?"

He raises his hand in surrender. His cheek already swelling and turning purple. It's a good thing we wear makeup for a living.

"Look, look. I was shielding her from seeing you with Nyx, but she already saw and drew her conclusion. You know why I gave her the rose. It's not like that."

"What did she say?" I ask.

"That she wishes she was part of it. We were all great, and she loved the circus. It was her first time seeing a show, and she has imagined being part of one since she was a little girl."

I see it in his eyes. There is more. "Go on," I urge.

His eyes dart to Nyx and then back. "She looked… disappointed. As much as she thought my performance was the best and loved the show, I know she won't be back."

"Your…performance," I say with disdain.

"Yeah, it was mine she liked the best," he says with pride and a busted lip.

I snort. "She was just being nice." But I know she meant it.

It was my performance I wanted her to like the best, but I fucked that up with her seeing me with Nyx.

Nyx walks up to Keir with a first-aid kit.

"Don't ever pull that stunt with me again," I warn her.

"I'm sorry, Draco. I wasn't thinking," she says with hurt in her eyes.

I have myself to blame. Nyx has been in love with me since I saved her all those years ago, but there is only one I want. The one I've been waiting for since I was six years old.

Her name is Ivy.

I tried to tell myself it wasn't her. It couldn't be, but I knew when I saw her with her dark-haired friend. It was real—all of it. I had my doubts but I felt it. I recognized it. I felt her everywhere.

When I held her on the ride, I knew. I knew it even if I denied it a hundred times. Even when I tried to fuck it out of me using Nyx and the others. But nothing worked.

"Go after her," Nyx says while tending to Keir.

"What am I supposed to do? Show up dressed like a ringmaster and sweep her off her feet?"

Her eyes lift. "Maybe…work for it… show her you want her." She pats Keir's cut, and I watch him wince. Shame washed over me for hitting him, but I had to stop him. "Get her to come." She throws back her head and laughs at her own joke.

I roll my eyes but feel my cock thicken, imagining Ivy coming on my tongue.

"I like her name. Ivy Sloan," Keir says.

"Ivy Sloan," Nyx says, testing her name on her tongue. "I love it! It's hot…she's hot," she continues in a syrupy voice, "I want to taste Ivy Sloan."

"Don't get ahead of yourself, Nyx," I warn.

"What…" She pouts dramatically. "You should see her swallow, Draco. She closes her eyes in pleasure, and all I can picture is Ivy Sloan swallowing my cum after she sucks my cock."

Lex walks in and looks at Keir. "Let me guess, he went near her." She walks up to the Butcher seated on a chair, straddles his lap, and looks directly at me. "She's jealous of Nyx. I saw it on her face when we were in the dungeon. It's why she stormed off."

The dungeon is our sex room. A room we have strictly for our VIPs who pay to watch, and we perform. It brings in twenty million a year in the States alone. It's growing. But we cap off how many tickets we sell, or this wouldn't be a circus.

"She's not jealous. She was disappointed," Keir points out.

"Of what?" the Butcher asks.

"Of not being part of it," Keir replies.

"Which part?" Lex asks with a smirk.

"All of it."

AFTER NONSTOP SHOWS, Devil's Night looms, keeping my mind off my blond temptress. I walk into my RV, sit on the couch, and place my top hat on the seat.

My phone goes off, and it's a text.

L: What hunts a rabbit no one thinks about when they go hunting?

Draco: That's easy, humans. I taught you that one.

L: What hunts a human and buys food at the grocery store?

Draco: Another human trying to save the rabbit.

L: Why would a human hunt a rabbit?"

My hand tightens around my phone, digging in my palm.

Draco: To eat wild game or keep them as pets.

L: Some pets don't like to be caged, but they stay caged because they don't have a choice.

I lock my phone and get up to take a cold shower.

Humans do not have natural-born predators unless they step out of their environment or...take something someone else wants.

Chapter Sixteen

I'M AT THE REGISTER, and it's twenty minutes after my shift is over. As I suspected, Kevin keeps me past sunset. The look in his eye when Trisha gave me a ride last week after I snubbed his offer was all I needed to know.

He would do anything to force me to accept his offer for a ride to get me alone. He thinks I will fold because of the news. They haven't found who's behind abducting and killing those girls. It has caused an uproar in the media. The poor victim's parents want answers. They want justice for their girls.

Trisha gives me an apologetic look, stocking the candy shelves in my lane.

She can't take me home today after my shift because her mother refuses to watch her kids later than necessary. Her mother was upset about the last time she agreed to give me a ride to the fair.

"I can take you home if you need a ride, Ivy," Kevin says, passing by the bagging area on his way to his office.

"That's okay. I got it sorted," I reply, wiping down the scanner.

His face falls, and I grin with satisfaction when he turns around. His plan didn't work. I would rather walk in the dark than sit in a car with him. Who knows what else he has up his sleeve, and I don't want to find out. I've dealt with enough creeps hanging around my mother back in South Carolina. Kevin has the same predatory look in his eye as they did.

I need to figure something out. I know I can't walk home on the main highway. It isn't safe, and it would be stupid. My mother gets off at midnight, so calling her isn't an option. I can't leave early because I need the money. I'm pondering the issue when my answer walks in my lane.

Dean.

"Hey, Ivy." He glances at Kevin as he walks back. "How are you doing, Kevin? How's the wife?"

"She's good." He looks at Dean, sizing him up. "Aren't you dating—"

"No. I'm not."

"Oh…I heard different."

Dean sighs, placing a TV dinner on the belt. "Nope. I'm single and ready for what life throws at me. I thought you would be having kids by now, Kevin."

"I don't like kids and not with this job. I work a lot of hours. You run a business. You can understand that."

"I hear ya." Dean pushes the cart down the lane but raises a brow at Trisha because he can't get through with the shopping cart.

Trisha places the gums and the chocolate bars as fast as she can to free her hands. She tries to squeeze in the space between the candy shelf and the next register to let Dean through.

"Get out of the way, Trisha. He's obviously waiting

for you to move. He can't fit with you there," Kevin reprimands, insinuating that she's fat.

Embarrassment crosses her features. She grabs the cardboard candy box and looks away. Kevin is such an asshole to her. I hate that he treats her like that.

"It's alright, Kevin. Dean can get through."

It's a tight fit, but he could. Dean is being an asshole like Kevin. Sometimes I wonder who's the biggest one.

Kevin glares at me. "Oh, aren't you the BFF trying to defend her. She's in the way." He opens his arms wide around his waist. "There is no way he could squeeze through with her there."

"She's stocking the candy aisle. Her hands were full, and she was about done. He could get through. There's enough space. You don't have to be so crude about it," I say in a hard tone.

He's pissed off because I won't let him give me a ride home, and his plan didn't work by getting me to stay late.

"Excuse me, miss?" An older woman walks up behind Dean, trying to get Trisha's attention. Her face is wrinkled from age with a worried expression.

"Yes," Trisha asks.

"A big spill in aisle four needs to be cleaned up. I would have slipped if the bottles hadn't been strewn across the floor and gotten stuck on the wheel of my cart."

"How did that happen?" Kevin asks her accusingly.

"I wouldn't know. There was a crash, but it wasn't loud. I was shopping for some wine, and then I saw it. The floor was painted crimson from all the broken bottles of red wine pouring out across the floor. It looks like a bloodbath over there. Like I said, it needs to be cleaned up."

"I'll go check it out," Trish says, walking toward aisle four.

Kevin sighs. "I need to find the idiot who did it. Whoever did it, is going to pay for it." And storms off.

"Dick," I mutter.

I grab the TV dinners and pause. A crisp one-hundred-dollar bill sits near the scanner. A dead president staring at me. Shame and anger bubble inside me. I look up. Dean is watching me.

"I know you need it, Ivy. The same way I know you need a ride home. The last shuttle left half an hour ago, and walking home is too dangerous. I'll give you a ride?"

I grip the cold paper carton over the plastic of his TV dinner causing it to crease. After heating it in the microwave, I know macaroni and cheese tastes like dried-up cardboard. Not even salt can fix the taste.

The same way the hundred-dollar bill staring at me won't fix the sick feeling of Dean fucking me over his kitchen island with his small dick.

My mother was right about me, and I refused to believe her. I was a little girl fantasizing about the circus because I wanted to be part of something great. I want to go somewhere different. But I'm not part of anything, and the show must go on. This is my show, and this is part of my act.

I convince myself I need the money to help pay the rent, or my mother will kick me out. I convince myself I need a ride home from Dean so I don't walk alone in the dark.

I hate Dean, but I hate myself more because I don't have a choice.

"Alright."

"Atta girl," he says and places a box of MyOne condoms near the scanner. Size small.

SITTING IN DEAN'S TRUCK, I clutch my bag in my lap like a lifesaver that will keep me from drowning. I convinced myself that I had no choice but to accept what was coming for me. My shame for his pleasure. Every dose costs me one hundred dollars.

The road is dark when he pulls out of the parking lot of the Big H. His house is not far. It's only a couple of blocks, but I wish it wasn't.

He reaches out and touches the screen to play music. The Doors "I Love Her Madly" plays. My head whips in his direction.

"Have you ever heard of The Doors?" he asks. He turns up the volume slightly, making me cringe. "It's not your time or mine, but my father listened to them."

He picks Jim Morrison's voice out of all the artists to play. How ironic. He's a sick fuck.

Especially when the song changes to "Touch Me."

"I know of them," I respond dryly, hating him even more.

I won't tell him I've listened to them on the radio. My mother likes The Doors. She started working at diners that played oldie tunes on the jukebox. Since then, they stuck.

She would find the radio station in her old sedan when she would take me to school that played them. Most people nowadays don't listen to the radio and instead stream from a music app, but I didn't have the option on my mother's radio. It was the only way you could listen to music. I welcomed it when she drove me to school or the store. It was better than static or her talking.

"It's one of my favorites." He glances at me briefly. "You know I still want you, Ivy."

I grip the strap to my bag in a tight fist. My stomach in knots. "I can't stop thinking about you when I'm with someone else." He lets out a laugh, and I want to throw up. "I've wanted your tight cunt since I first laid eyes on you when you were seventeen. I tried to tell myself I was crazy, but I couldn't resist. I couldn't resist wanting to fuck your tight pink cunt, but I had to wait until you were eighteen." I look out the window, trying to blink back the sting from my eyes when I'm thrown forward. Tires squeal, and rocks hit metal. I place my hand on the dash to keep from hitting my head on the windshield and push back on the seat.

"What the fuck!" Dean yells as he blares the horn.

CHAPTER SEVENTEEN

A SATIN-BLACK PLYMOUTH BARRACUDA blocks Dean's truck. The windows are tinted so dark you could see the moon's reflection.

Dean blares his horn again, causing me to jolt. "Piece of shit. You fucking psycho!" Dean yells like the person inside the car can hear him.

My hands shake from the adrenaline running through my veins. Dean looks out the truck's rear window, but we're blocked in by the trees at an angle that he can't back up.

The Plymouth engine roars so loud it blocks out the music inside the truck. Dean turns the wheel and moves the car forward but applies the brake. There is no room to drive away without hitting the car.

I focus on the driver's side door, waiting to see who steps out. A second turns into what seems like minutes. I hold my breath, contemplating opening my door to run, but where would I go. How far would I get? I let out a shaky breath and lick my dry lips.

"Motherfucker," Dean spits. The vein in his neck bulges. "Who does this motherfucker think he is?" He opens his door.

"I don't think that's a good idea, Dean."

She glares at me. "Shut up. You stupid bitch."

I lean against my door, clutching my bag, and point behind him. My insides churn with dread, a cold knot forming at the pit of my stomach.

A man dressed all in black with a white mask is there.

He turns around, and the man grips his hair. "Ahh-hh!" Dean cries.

"You should have listened to her, Dean," the man says in a raspy voice, dragging him out of the car. Dean tries to swing at him but fails to connect, instead flaring his arms around.

I place my hands over my mouth because I know it's him. I know it's Draco.

"Let me go, you son of a bitch!" Dean yells, trying to get out of Draco's hold.

Draco laughs at his failed attempts.

He bends and looks at me. "Get out."

I open the door, scramble out, not caring the weeds scratch my ankles, and stop in front of the car. I squint from the glare of the headlights, looking down the dark road. He'll catch me if I run. He'll hurt me if I call for help. But who do I need help *from*?

I look back. Draco slams Dean on the hood of his truck, pulling him by the hair so Dean can look at me with his eyes bulging. "Don't you think she's too young for you?"

"Fuck you," Dean snarls.

"You didn't answer my question."

He slams his forehead on the hood. "Fuck!" Dean grunts.

"Let's try again. You like to fuck young girls. You like to take advantage of them."

"What the fuck are you talking about?"

"Look at her," Draco demands. "Are you paying to fuck her?"

"Fuck off!"

Draco slams his head again, denting the hood. When he pulls his head back, big fat drops of blood splatter on the hood. "What the hell, man! You busted my face. Who are you? What the fuck do you want?"

"I'm getting to that, but you won't answer my questions. Let's start over. Are you paying to fuck her?"

"Yes," Dean admits in a strangled voice.

"Hmm…how long?"

"Two years. How old is she?"

"Eighteen."

I'm nineteen, but it wouldn't matter to someone like him. I could be fifteen to someone like Dean, and he still would have done it.

"So you like to fuck underaged girls…prey on the weak and underprivileged. Groom them for your pathetic cock because it's too small."

"Why the fuck do you care? So what, I fucked her. What the fuck is it to you?"

Draco answers with a bone-chilling laugh. "One last question, and I'll let you go." Fear twists in my gut like a coiled serpent, sending waves of nausea through me. "What runs and runs but can never flee? It is often watched yet never seen. When short, it brings fear. What is it?" Dean struggles, but Draco's hold is too strong, and he can't move. It doesn't help Dean that Draco towers over him or that his face is full of blood from the gash on his forehead. "I'm waiting," Draco singsongs. "Come on, you can do it. It's not that hard." Draco leans close to

Dean's bloody face, staining his white mask. "Your freedom depends on it."

"I–I—"

Draco makes a buzzard sound, lifting his head, and then says, "Look at her, Dean," in a flat voice.

"A hamster," Dean says with terror in his eyes.

"Time of death," Draco corrects.

DRACO SLAMS the door after sliding into the passenger side of his black Plymouth. I try to look out the side mirror but can't determine if he is going to Dean's truck. But I have my answer when the driver's side door opens, and he gets in.

The interior of his car is black with shiny black dials. It's immaculate and smells of rich leather and his scent—citrus, woodsy, and dark like the man. The car vibrates from the massive engine, drowning out the music coming from Dean's car. The air was cool outside, but I was so scared, I didn't notice.

He removes the white mask, and from the corner of my eye, I see his straight nose, full lips, and black hair the same color as his car. His skin is smooth despite wearing makeup all the time.

"Are you going to hurt me?" I ask.

It's a stupid question, but I had to ask. I saw what he did to Dean, but I also saw what he did to Paul and Jason at school.

He doesn't answer and presses the touch screen,

which is obviously aftermarket. He grabs his phone from the holder he has installed near the black and white gauges.

A loud thump can be heard coming from the trunk.

I glance at him. His midnight eyes meet mine, hellishly bright and aware, and I'm lost under his spell.

He selects a song and places his phone back on the holder. Depeche Mode's "Enjoy the Silence" plays. The engine roars, adding to the background of the music, as he drives down the road.

I see the bright lights of the fair. The Ferris wheel to the right of the carnival with rainbow lights fading in and out, and the one to the right with its dark red lights and swinging gondolas.

He pulls around back down a dark road. The man manning the gate recognizes his car. He tilts his head and nods when he spots Draco behind the wheel and waves him through.

The road is paved. There are no potholes or rocks. Three red-and-white circus tents are to my right, large and imposing. The car moves at a slow pace and stops behind the tent farthest to the back.

The song changes to "Mouth" by Bush. He turns it up to drown out the noise from the back.

He places the car in park in front of a luxury RV. He glances at me for a beat, then leaves the car on, gets out, and closes the door.

I'm considering getting out, but where would I go? Is he kidnapping me? It wouldn't be kidnapping if I stayed. Right?

A sinking feeling stabs at my core. Is he the killer? I

look out the back window when the car rocks, but I can't see anything but the trunk open.

He would have killed me. There is no way he would bring me back to the fairgrounds. There are people. I could scream and call for help.

The trunk slams, and I jolt.

The passenger door opens, and the interior light flicks on. He grabs me gently by the arm and pulls me out.

I move to the side and lean with my back against the car. The curtain from the tent falls closed, and I know that's where they took Dean.

Draco leans inside the car, grabs his keys, shuts off the music, and closes the door. He steps close, and I tilt my head back, lifting my chin. He's fucking tall. Six foot six at least to my five-four. He's wearing a black hoodie that does nothing to hide his broad frame. A tattoo that reads DRACO in big letters is written across his thick neck with flames underneath.

His eyes land on my name tag on the vest of my uniform. He lifts the tag with black-painted nail polish on his fingernails.

"It says Ivy," I say, like he doesn't know how to read.

His eyes lift, like dark liquid pools. He drops his hand, walks to the RV, and pulls the door open.

I walk cautiously up the steps. The inside is pure luxury. LED lights line the floors and ceiling. Black leather covers the seats. There are three television sets with speakers in the living room. The kitchen has a black stainless steel convection microwave oven, a two-burner induction stove, a residential-size refrigerator, and a dish-washer. It even has an electric fireplace with white marble floors. It smells like the perfume section in the department store inside the mall. Expensive.

"Is this where you live?" I ask. He shuts the door and walks to the back. "Are you going to keep ignoring me?"

He opens a door that leads to a bathroom with a spa. It's bigger than the bathroom in my apartment. He removes his black hoodie. He isn't wearing a shirt underneath. His hard body ripples with muscle and tattoos.

My eyes trail down the waves of ab muscles disappearing to the deep V in the waistband of his pants.

"Do you want to take a shower?" he asks.

He speaks.

"I don't…think… that's a good idea. Are you going to kill him?"

I had to ask. I would tell him to take me home. I don't want to shower…I do, but not like this. With him, maybe, but…

"Do you want me to?" He walks toward me slowly, and I can't tear my eyes from his gorgeous body. I can't think around him. His face reminds me of River Phoenix with black hair and dark eyes with the body of a tattooed model.

Get a grip, Ivy. Answer.

"I hate him, but I don't think he deserves to die."

"What do you think he deserves?"

I shake my head slowly. "I don't know."

His eyes caress my face, and I want to melt.

"Did he force you? Did he…touch you when you said no."

I shake my head and look away. "No. He figured out a way so I wouldn't *say* no."

"Are you a whore? Do you sell your pussy for money?"

The letters carved in the wooden desks and written on the walls at school float in my mind. IVY SLOAN IS A SLUT. The one-hundred-dollar bill Dean would give me after he was done.

Draco must think I'm pathetic and asked for it, and is one of the reasons I'm asking him not to kill Dean. Why Jason and Paul thought they could rape me at school. The reason I'm ogling him without his shirt hoping to get something more out of him.

He assumes the same thing all men do when they look at me. I can't tell him no because I have had sex for money. Not because I wanted to but because it was the only way I could survive. A reason he wouldn't understand. Ugly shame spreads like a rash over my skin, reminding me of what I am.

The door swings open, saving me from answering, and it's the girl I saw him with inside the sex room.

She's gorgeous without her clown makeup.

"Oh…" She looks nervously at Draco. "I—"

"It's not what you think," I rush out. Guilt rises to the surface. He doesn't have a shirt on. I'm alone with him, and it looks bad. "I was just leaving."

She steps farther inside but doesn't say anything.

I walk out the small door, purposely avoiding Draco glad I have a good reason to leave.

I can hear them talking inside but can't make out what they are saying, and I don't want to be the cause of them fighting.

I almost reach the back gate when a familiar voice stops me. "Why every time I find you, you're leaving?"

Keir.

"Because you have bad timing," I tease.

"Do I?"

I turn to face him with a smirk. He's wearing black-and-white-striped pants and a matching shirt. It's unbuttoned and looks more like a jacket over his hard body.

I smile because his makeup is amusing. His mouth is painted, giving the illusion of being unnaturally wide with white and black face paint and red shading.

"Did you just perform?"

"No. I was practicing and tending to other stuff."

He means Dean.

"I was heading home," I say.

He looks out the gate. "On foot?"

"It's all I got."

I can't tell him I have a hundred bucks I can't spend on an Uber.

A generator turns on behind him. The smell of barbecue rolls in from the food trucks at the fair.

"Are you hungry? Because I am…it will be my treat."

"Don't you have a girlfriend somewhere?"

He laughs. "I don't, and neither does anyone else here. Maybe Butcher, but I don't know his deal yet."

"Oh…I thought—"

"Nyx isn't Draco's girlfriend."

"Oh…I didn't—"

"You don't have to say it, Ivy. I can see it, and so can everyone else."

"I don't know what you're talking about," I say defensively.

Her name is Nyx. It's cool, and…it fits.

She isn't his girlfriend, but they fuck. That part is

obvious, and he thinks I'm a whore. Perfect. He wouldn't have asked if he didn't assume.

"I really should get going."

His expression turns to disappointment, making him look funny because of the makeup.

"What's so funny?"

I didn't realize I was grinning. I thought I was doing it in my head.

"I—"

"Do you always run away when someone asks you a question?"

I turn around, and Draco is wearing a black hoodie, with Nyx at his side.

She rolls her eyes and steps forward. "Hi, I'm Nyx," she introduces herself with a naughty smile.

"Ivy."

Her smile widens, and her eyes land on my name tag. "The Big H, huh."

"Yeah, they were the only ones hiring."

Her eyes slide to Draco and then to Keir. "Keir, I need you to help me with something on stage."

I could tell she doesn't and is trying to get me alone with Draco. "Alright." Keir gives me a wink walking backwards pointing at me. "Don't leave. One of us can take you home." He walks away with his arm around Nyx's waist, disappearing inside the tent.

"Come with me," Draco demands.

"Why?"

"Because I know you're hungry, and we both know I'm not going to let anyone who isn't me take you home."

"On one condition..." His eyes narrow. "If you let

Dean go. It wouldn't be good if he disappeared after people saw me leaving with him."

"Alright, but not until I'm done with him. If he goes near you again… his time is up."

I follow him to his car trying to keep up with his long strides. "What do you mean his time is up."

He opens the door and takes out a gray hoodie. "Here," he says, "it's cold."

It is cold. Every day, it gets colder as the fall season settles in. At night, it drops ten or fifteen degrees.

"Where are you taking me?"

"To eat…" I pull the sweater over my breasts, his eyes fixed on the little hole the middle button makes when my shirt pulls. His eyes lift. "I'm hungry."

CHAPTER EIGHTEEN
DRACO

HOW DO you get a woman to like you when you have never had that problem all your life? I should have never asked her if she sold her pussy for money. It was fucked up. She ran out the door.

Nyx showing up didn't help the cause. I wanted to kick her out of my RV but held back. I didn't miss the look of hurt in her eyes when she saw how I looked at Ivy, but I told her the truth.

Accept it or leave.

She stayed.

I admit I was showing off by taking my sweater off when I asked if she wanted a shower. I wanted to see her in my clothes and wearing the scent of my soap on her skin.

I panicked when she was almost to the back gate with Keir afraid of her leaving or him saying something to her that would have her running. I want to know what he said to her but first, I need to feed my little rabbit. She looks tired, hungry and scared.

"Pick a side," I tell her, extending my arms when we reach the crossroads. "The left is dark, and the right is light."

She looks indecisive. Her eyes darted left and right, but surprises me when she says, "Dark."

"Good choice."

I go left, past the entrance, and walk through the gate, bypassing security. She follows me by the employee's side, avoiding the fog. You can hear people screaming from the actors startling them.

"It's different when you're the one scaring them, right?" she asks.

I can see her point. It is different.

"Yes, it's fun if you're into it."

"Are you…into it?"

I pause and stare for a second too long. "I'm always into it. I like to perform."

I like the way my gray sweater swallows her petite body. I wonder how she tastes. If her pussy is as pink as that bastard said it was. I grind my teeth, wanting to rip his arms off for touching her. I take a deep breath and remind myself, in time.

"So what would you like to eat? I tried the bucket of meat kabobs that looked like guts and the smoking blood from the guy wearing the jester costume. That was good."

I smile. The way she talks about the food I selected for the park is amusing. "Have you tried the gelato brains? They are my personal favorite."

She giggles, and the sound sings to the head of my cock. I want to fuck her. I want to fuck her hard. She has nice tits and a nice ass, and I bet the motherfucker is right about her cunt being tight. I want to sink my teeth into it and make her scream. I want to make her bleed from the marks I make on her skin. I bet her blood tastes sweet.

"I haven't." She's so small, I hope I don't break her. "Hey, a-are you okay?"

I tilt my head to catch her gaze. "Huh?"

"You were staring at…nothing," she says worriedly.

I want to break you.

"How loud do you scream?" I ask.

"W-why would you ask me that?"

"Curious. You can tell a lot about the way a person screams."

"How loud do you scream?" she volleys back.

We stop at the food truck. The smell of barbecue floats around us, mixing with the cool air like clouds of smoke. The generators are loud on this side.

"When I kill." I smile when I see the look of terror in her eyes. My cock thickens inside my boxers. "But I'm silent when I fuck."

"How can I help…" Thomas pops his head out, catching the wig on the window's edge. He smooths it down and adjusts it. "How can I help you?" he tries again.

He spots me behind Ivy, and his eyes widen despite the stupid clown costume he's wearing. His makeup is all wrong, cracking near the collar of his clown costume. I don't like it.

Ivy scans the menu from the chalkboard hanging on the side of the truck. "I'll have the human ribs with fingers."

His red nose falls off and floats on the pavement.

"Shit," he mutters, cupping his nose with his palm like it will magically reappear.

"Bad day?" I ask Thomas.

Ivy chases the red nose. She catches it and hands it to him. "Here, you lost this," she says with a laugh.

He takes it and pushes it back on his pointy nose. It's most likely why it won't stay on.

"What do you say?" I tell Thomas like I'm teaching a small child manners.

"Right." Thomas says, "Thank you—"

"Ivy, and you are?"

"Bozo," I answer for him.

She laughs, but I don't. I'm staring at *can't get right Thomas*. He's always fucking up. Comes high to work all the time and screws up everyone's order, and his makeup looks like shit.

"It's Thomas," he corrects.

"It's Bozo," I counter.

He sighs heavily and glances at Ivy. "It's Bozo."

She glances at me and then at Bozo. "Nice to meet you, Bozo. Looks like you need to freshen up."

Good. She sees it, too. He's a mess.

"Make that two of whatever she orders."

"Yes, sir."

We sit, and I watch her eat. How her tongue licks her lips and the sauce off her fingers makes me imagine something else.

"Aren't you going to eat?"

I grab her wrist and bring her fingers to my mouth. She sucks in a breath when the tip of my tongue glides between her index and middle finger, and then I suck.

I close my eyes, savoring the taste of her skin and the barbecue sauce. "Mm…"

She tastes sweet and spicy. I want to lick it all.

She whimpers when I suck the last of the sauce off her thumb. When my eyes open, she's watching me, her eyes the color of dark honey. Hot and full of secrets.

We all have secrets. We all have fears. Wants. Needs. Desires.

I want all of hers, but mine she will fear.

"WHAT MADE you want to be in a circus?"

What made you want to fuck losers? But I don't ask her that. I'm sure she has a reason. We all have reasons that make us do things. I turn the heater on in the car to take her home. It's almost midnight.

"I was born to be in a circus. I knew since I learned to walk and what a clown was."

"Most kids are afraid of clowns."

"I wanted to be the clown."

"I can see that," she says.

"Can you?"

"I saw you perform. It was…powerful."

"Did you like it?"

"I loved the main show."

Not disappointed.

"You didn't like the other show?" I press.

She glances at me, clutching her bag to her chest. "I didn't stay to watch."

"I didn't stay to perform," I admit.

"Why not?"

I shouldn't have told her, and I don't know why I did. I didn't fuck Nyx, and she didn't suck my dick. I couldn't.

"I wasn't supposed to be there."

"Oh…" She trails off when I pull into her apartment complex. A run-down shithole full of assholes one paycheck away from getting evicted. I don't want to leave her here, but I don't have a choice.

Soon.

"How come you work at the Big H?" I ask.

"It's just my mom and me, and we need the money."

Typical single mom and daughter story. Where the daughter needs to help the mom because the mom can't figure shit out on her own. Probably makes her feel guilty too.

"How come you were in the bathroom at school?"

"Someone I know goes there."

"Who——"

"It's getting late."

"Thanks for dinner and for not…" She pauses. "You know what I mean. Promise me?"

I glance at her. "I'll do my best."

She shuts the door, and I wait, watching her hips sway up the stairs.

I drive to the back, where I have a clear view of her entering her apartment. Number 206. But I knew that.

Back in the tent, the red light shines on Dean's pathetic form, seated in the chair. He's blindfolded, gagged, and tied by his hands and feet. Nyx stands behind him with a jagged knife in her hands.

I give her the signal to remove the gag. "If you scream or yell, I'll slice your fucking throat," I warn.

I will anyway, but he doesn't know that.

"What do you want?" He asks in a hoarse voice.

Funny he doesn't ask about Ivy. I could have killed her, and he wouldn't have cared.

"I want you to stay away from Ivy. I don't want you around her. I suggest you start ordering your groceries online. Move your business to another state. Give you a head start."

"Are you fucking serious? For a girl? She's no one."

I tilt my head slowly to Nyx. She slaps him with the flat part of the knife across his face.

"Ow!" he howls.

Pathetic.

I step forward cautiously, not wanting to smell him. It's what she's had to smell, and it's an unsettling sensation that turns my stomach.

"I'm going to cut you up and feed you to tigers."

"You're a circus clown." He laughs. "You're part of the Ringling Brothers."

I signal to Nyx. She hits him harder, slicing his face this time.

He howls again.

"Are you done insulting my family? They don't like to be compared."

He is about to respond but hesitates from the pain. Blood drips down his chin.

"You cut me."

"That's how it starts."

"What starts?"

He's nervous. His hands are shaking.

"The time of your death."

"You were serious about that?"

"I never joke when I kill. It's bad manners."

He struggles to pull his hands and feet free. It's amusing.

When he's done, he is out of breath and sweating profusely.

"Like I said, you should find another way to shop and conduct your business of cleaning shit. Have you ever heard of *'you don't shit where you eat'* ? I'm the first one to tell you it's bad practice. It *will* kill you."

"You're crazy."

"I prefer to identify myself as insane, but you're not qualified to make that determination. You'll find out when do kill you."

The things I want to do to this man with a hammer and a bone cutter.

"You're going to kill me."

"I am." Why lie? "But not tonight. I like to hunt my kill. I want you to run. I want your fear. I want to see how pathetic you'll look when you avoid the grocery store."

"Why? Why do you want to kill me?"

"You know why. I'm going to drop you off at your pathetic excuse of a white truck. You'll go home and forget any of this happened. If you go near the grocery store or Ivy, I'll cut your eyes out and drain your bodily fluids. Do you understand me?"

He nods frantically.

Keir walks in. "Take him back," I tell him after sending him a text with the location of his truck.

I glance at Nyx and nod for her to begin.

I close my eyes and hear his screams after I shut the door.

I find Lex near the back door behind one of the haunted houses. "Where are you going?" she asks.

"Where I've been going for the past month."

Lex is a gorgeous redhead with long legs and an incredible mouth. She's fun to watch, but there is a blonde I'm dying to see.

"Teach her."

I look back before walking out. "I will, but I need to break her first."

"She's already broken, Draco."

"How so?"

Lex has an eye for these things. She sees things others don't. It's been that way for a long time.

"Nyx was taken by force, and we saved her. Ivy had no choice and accepted what she's had to do." She pushes off the door. "She's already broken, Draco. If you push, you will lose her."

"You're wrong, Lex. She will be what she is destined to become."

CHAPTER NINETEEN

I'M SITTING on the roof of my apartment building wearing a sweater, black leggings, and a gray blanket I found for five dollars at Dollar General on clearance. I take a seat on the lawn chair I found behind the dumpster and look at the white rectangular screen, waiting for Stephen King's *It* to start.

Not many cars are out tonight. Just a couple of kids from school with fogged-up windows fucking. I spot a couple of cheerleaders with some of the football players from school. I recognize their cars; about four or five are parked in the back row, leaving one row with enough space so the other eight cars up front don't see what they are doing from their rearview mirror.

I was relieved I saw Dean's truck with dirt smudged all over the side this morning when I got into work. Draco didn't kill him, or maybe he was bluffing, but I doubt it. He didn't walk in the grocery store because he probably freaked out. He wouldn't give a shit if I was dead or alive.

No more convincing me to give me a ride.

Those guys at the Circus of Freaks are into other shit I don't want to find out. Dark and dangerous.

The credits roll in as the movie starts.

"Is this your favorite?"

A shiver dances down my spine, and it's not from the cold wind. Draco stands like a looming shadow next to me. The yellow glow from the streetlight by the dumpster makes his shadow stretch to the edge of the building.

"Do you always sneak up on women?" I ask, my heart pounding in my chest.

"No…just you." His voice echoes in my head.

I wake up panting. I look around, and then I hear it. My is alarm going off. I silence my phone and check the time. 9:00 a.m. I fall back on my pillow looking at the ceiling.

It was a dream, Ivy.

I didn't see *It* last night. They don't play horror movies on Wednesdays. Only Thursdays. And Draco didn't show up, and my blanket is in the basket needing to be washed.

"Ivy?" My mother opens my bedroom door. "Are you taking me to work today? If you are, we gotta go now, but remember, you can't pick me up late."

Since I'm working full time this week, my mother has been nice and offered me the car. She's hoping I ditch school and keep working. It's her way to convince me to drop out. She doesn't know I'm planning on going back on Monday.

I sit up. "Yeah, I'll be ready in a minute."

After dropping my mother off at the Moonlight Diner, I head toward the Big H for my shift in her beat-up clunker.

There's another alert on my phone. Another girl missing, Jenny Carson. Seventeen years old. Last seen outside the mall three towns over. More girls have gone missing and found dead.

No leads.

Whoever is doing it knows how to cover their tracks.

When I pull into the parking lot of the plaza of the Big H, I notice a huge sign in front of DTF that says, Moving Sale.

There's some good news.

"Hey, Ivy," Trisha greets me with a beaming smile on her rosy cheeks. "Got yourself some wheels?"

"No. I wish…it's my mom's," I clarify. "She let me borrow it to get to work until I have to get back to school on Monday."

"Oh…well…at least you have a ride now."

After my shift at the Big H, I was relieved when Dean didn't show up. I head out in my mom's old clunker toward the diner. I turn the radio on. The oldie station it's set to plays The Angels "My Boyfriend's Back."I sing along, surprisingly knowing the words like I've been playing it my whole life.

I turn it up and sway to the music.

The sun has set by the time I walk inside the diner with my mom's car keys in hand.

"Hey, Maggy!" Joan shouts from the back. "Your daughter is here." She gives me a wan smile. "Hey, baby. Sorry, but it's gonna be a while."

I look around, and it's a full house on a Thursday night. I'm surprised. My mom told me business has been slow.

"That's alright, Joan. I'll wait."

"How's school? Heard you got suspended." She gives me a wink. "Giving those boys trouble."

"No," I reply in a flat tone.

Joan is an older version of my mom. It's why they get along. Both come from a small town with a shitty upbringing working at diners and gas stations all their life.

I sit on the stool by the counter and watch my mom flirt with a man seated in booth eight. He's heavy set with a trucker hat and scruff on his face. The rig parked out front must be his. He nods at whatever my mother is telling him while staring at the other server's ass. I think her name is Cynthia. She doesn't have an ass by any means, but compared to my mom and Joan, she's the best-looking server here.

"What's your name, darlin'?" I shift in the seat and turn to look at a man with brown hair and a beard.

"Who wants to know?"

I know his type. He likes girls who are barely legal. I took my name tag off my uniform before entering to avoid anyone knowing my name. Moonlight Diner attracts truckers, tourists, and travelers who come through. Mostly sleazy assholes like the one I'm looking at right now.

"My name's John."

He's lying. I catch the white tan line of his ring finger. No one is stupid enough to give out their real name when they are trying to hide the fact they are married.

"I'm Jane."

He chuckles at my obvious bluff. "Jane."

I raise a brow. "John?"

"What do you say we get out of here? I know a nice drive-in not too far from here."

I laugh.

He smiles, but it doesn't reach his eyes. "What's so funny?"

"You expect me to go somewhere with you?"

"Why not? I know your mother works here."

I glance at Joan, but she's busy pulling tickets and fixing plates for customers to notice John sitting next to me.

John's a creep.

I slide off the stool. "Where you goin'?"

Ignoring him, I walk to the women's restroom.

I use the toilet, wash my hands, and fix my hair. When I walk out, I'm blocked by John waiting for me right outside the hallway of the restroom. "You didn't answer me, Jane. How about that drive-in?"

I act like I didn't hear him and go around him, but he blocks me.

"What the fuck, John? The answer is no. Now fuck off."

His nostrils flare, and his eyes are pitch black. His nose is slightly crooked. This close, he looks to be in his late thirties, maybe early forties.

"Well, that's not very nice."

"Neither is some middle-aged creep that can't take the fucking hint when a lady isn't interested. Now move."

He leers at me for a few seconds. My stomach lurches in fear. "Yeah, you're the hard-to-get type who needs a little persuasion." He lowers his voice. "Your mom told me about her pretty daughter who looks just like her when she was young, and we both know your name isn't Jane."

Tears burn my eyes.

I push him out of the way, then march toward my mother and slam the keys on the table of booth eight. "Ivy—"

"I'll find a ride home." And I storm out of the diner.

I swipe furiously at the tears that have escaped and lean on the wall where no one can see me.

"Why does she have to be so stupid," I mumble.

Why can't she be a normal mother? How could she talk about me like that to a complete stranger? It's obvious she gave him more than just service at the diner.

I didn't realize I was walking toward the back of the building when I someone asks, "You need a ride?"

It's John.

"No."

"It looks like you do."

"I don't. Now leave me alone."

"See…I think you need a ride. A long one."

What the fuck is wrong with the men in this town?

I walk toward the back entrance of the diner and open the door. "I'll be here in case you change your mind."

"You had a better chance with my mother," I shoot back and walk inside.

I re-claim my seat at the counter. Joan looks up. "Sorry, babe, it's a busy night."

"I see that," I tell her, watching my mother. I don't mention John and I don't think she noticed me leave.

Joan opens the door to the carousel, rotating the desserts, and places a piece of cheesecake in front me. I look up, and she smiles. "It's on the house."

"Thanks, Joan."

She knows money is tight for Mother and me, and we can barely keep up with the bills.

After placing my fork down, feeling my stomach cramp from all the sugar, the cook with the apron rushes up to Joan. "Call 911, Joan. Now!"

"What now, Bruce?" she says, placing the dish towel on the counter.

Bruce's eyes have a look of horror. "Tell them to come out back. Blue Ford, Joan. Tell them to send the coroner," he says, out of breath.

"What the hell is going on?" Joan says grabbing the phone.

I slide off the stool and rush out the back door by the bathroom, then pause. Three guys surround the driver's side door, but I hear a familiar song playing on the radio. The Angels "My Boyfriend's Back."

"Jesus,"one man says, gripping his gray hair.

"He was just inside. I saw him," another man with a red trucker hat says.

"His eyes."

I walk slowly. *The song.* All I hear is the song playing in my head.

My eyes go wide when I see John dead in the driver's side. His head on the seat tilted up. His eyes are missing. There is a white piece of paper with SHE HAD ME AT JANE written in his blood and stuck to his forehead. His throat cut. There is blood all over his shirt and the steering wheel.

I can hear the police sirens from a distance.

"Who's Jane?"

"Get her out of here?"

Someone touches my shoulder. It's Bruce.
"You're Maggy's daughter, right?"
"Huh?"
The song. The song.

CHAPTER TWENTY

AFTER THREE HOURS of police questioning everyone at the diner, we finally make it home. I can't get the song out of my head or what the note said.

When the cops questioned me, I didn't say anything. I didn't tell him I talked to him except when someone pointed out he was seated next to me at the counter. But all I said was that he knew I was Maggy Sloan's daughter to avoid any mention of the name Jane.

Since the diner is old, there are no working cameras.

"Are you alright?" my mother asks.

I don't mention what she said to him or how pissed off and disappointed I am in her. She is not going to change the way she is because of me. She would have a long time ago.

"I'm fine."

"Who knows if he had any enemies. He's a trucker and passes through from town to town. State to state. Some people have secrets they don't tell. Back home, it happened all the time. People owing drug dealers money. Druggies who couldn't handle their high," she says in her Southern accent. "You know that's the way of life, Ivy."

She doesn't want to admit that he pays for sex and is

a dirtbag. Probably does drugs. She probably slept with him for money. He's a piece of shit.

"What was his name?"

I know it's not John. He is a liar on top of a rapist.

"His name was Steven. All I know is that he was married and drove an eighteen-wheeler."

You knew him so well to give him information about your daughter and screw him for money. He could have a disease. He could have killed his wife or raped someone a few towns over. But I don't tell her that. There is no point in telling her anything because I think I know who killed Steven, and it has everything to do with me.

I PUSH the slot after placing the fifth quarter to start the wash. One drawback of living in an old apartment complex is the shared laundry facilities. I hate having to wait until I finish all the laundry. You can't walk away or people will steal your clothes by the time you come back.

I hop on the counter and scroll through my phone when a text pops up.

Unknown: It's not safe to be out at night.

Who the hell is this?

Ivy: Who is this?

Unknown: Guess

I look at the entry way but don't see anyone.

Ivy: It is also not safe to talk to strangers.

Unknown: True. But we are not strangers.

Ivy: Who is this?

Unknown: You didn't guess.

Ivy: You texted me.

Unknown: I did.

Ivy: Why?

Unknown: Because you're bored. Waiting sucks.

Fear drips down my spine. I jump off the counter and look out the empty hallway, afraid that someone could be hiding behind the wall on the left. I look at the concrete floor to see if I can see a shadow but there is no one. Whoever this is, knows where I am.

Unknown: You shouldn't be scared, Ivy. Look what happened to the last guy.

Ivy: Who the fuck is this?

"This isn't funny. I know you're there," I say in a shaky voice.

> Unknown: I am equally comfortable in your mouth and in your shoe. What am I ?

> Ivy: Stop it.

> Unknown: Wrong. A tongue.

It's him. The riddles. He likes to mess with people's heads.

> Ivy: What loses its head in the morning and gets it back at night?

> Unknown: Me. When Ivy touches my cock.

> Ivy: Very funny. A pillow.

The washing machine abruptly switches cycles with a mechanical clunk. Startled, I jolt, almost dropping my phone.

> Unknown: Have a seat and let's continue.

I hop on the counter.

> Ivy: Look at my back, I am no one. Look at my face, I am someone. What am I ?

> Unknown: Mine.

> Ivy: No. A mirror.

Unknown: Hm…I was hoping I got that one right.

Ivy: Impossible because I don't share.

Unknown: Jealous?

Ivy: I should ask you.

Unknown: Imagine if he touched you.

Ivy: What would you have done?

Unknown: I can't tell you all my secrets.

Ivy: Then I can't tell you mine.

Unknown: But I already know all your secrets, Ivy.

Anticipation claws at my skin, causing my heart to beat faster.

Ivy: What are they?

Unknown: If I told you, they wouldn't be secrets.

When the washer stops, I transfer the clothes to the dryer and notice he's stopped texting me.

Ivy: Where are you?

I check my phone every minute until the dryer stops, and it's time for me to leave.

He never answered.

I sit in the lawn chair on the roof. Like my dream last night, I stare at the square white screen from the drive-in and wait for the credits to start. Instead of Stephen King's *It*, it's *Friday the 13th*, the 2009 remake, which is the best remake in my opinion.

I grip the freshly washed warm blanket that smells like lavender from the dryer sheets I bought on clearance at the Big H. I hold the small radio to the station so I can hear the movie. This is how I spend my movie nights because we can't afford to pay monthly for streaming apps, a good TV, or purchase movies. When you've lived in a trailer most of your life, there wasn't much we came with.

"Is this how you watch scary movies?"

I jump in my seat. I look to my right, and Draco stands next to me, wearing black boots, jeans, and a black sweater with a leather jacket.

What the fuck?

It feels like déjà vu or my dream coming true. I'm not superstitious, but the fortune teller told me to listen to my dreams. Could she be for real?

"It's the only way I can," I admit. "I don't exactly own a car, and my mother is strict about letting me use hers."

"Have you gone to the drive-in?"

His voice is haunting and mesmerizing. A deep resonance with a hint of melancholy. It has me in his grip. I don't want to tell him the truth, but I can't seem to lie.

Not to him.

"Once."

"A date?"

"The first, worst, and last. I'll take my chances on this roof."

"That bad?"

I snort. "Nothing memorable…like everything I've experienced. First times are supposed to be unforgettable. In my case, I wished I could forget they ever happened."

"Your first was bad. Bad date? Bad fuck?"

I giggle. "You know, you could just ask me if it was when I lost my virginity."

"Are you a virgin?" I hear a hint of British in his voice.

I suck in a breath. "No."

"How was your first time?"

I look at him like he's lost his mind. His dark eyes meet mine, and I could tell he wants to know. Not because he's being nosy but because it matters to him. I won't tell him who it was. I'm sure his was better.

"When I first moved here, no one knew me…naturally. I come from a long generation of trailer trash. Every stigma of living at a trailer park, there is some truth in it. Anyway, I never had a guy pay attention to me before in the way it was supposed to be. People knew where I lived at my old school, and my mother had a better reputation with the fathers than with the mothers. When we moved here, I was asked out by one of the most popular guys at school. I was excited. I wanted to live the fantasy until they found out about me. I didn't think it would be a nightmare, but I wasn't thinking. I didn't think he would take me to the drive-in on a first date. Everyone knows you don't actually watch the movies at the drive-in. I thought he was a nice guy. "

"Did he hurt you?"

"No. His dick was small, the seat belt in the back seat of his Mustang hurt more than him popping my cherry, and he lasted three minutes."

"You didn't come?"

"No. I couldn't wait until he got off me."

"What happened after?"

"He told the whole school I was a slut."

"He didn't want everyone to know he has a two-inch dick."

"I guess. It doesn't change that it was bad."

"Have you ever had a good time?"

I smile. "Are you asking me if I've ever had good sex?"

He towers over me, the movie long forgotten. "Maybe I am." He pulls the blanket off slowly. "Can I take you somewhere?"

"Depends on where you plan on taking me."

"Somewhere unforgettable."

CHAPTER TWENTY-ONE

HE TURNS RIGHT, goes over an empty road by the beltway.

We're in the middle of nowhere. The moon hangs high in the dark sky. The breeze cause the trees to groan.

"Why are we here?"

He shuts the door to his car. "You'll see."

I get out of the car. "What are you going to do?"

He leans on the hood of his car. "What do you want me to do, Ivy?"

"I'm not sure. You asked me to go with you, so I did."

"Do you like me, Ivy?"

"I-I don't know you."

"Did you know your first, your last?"

"Not in the way it counts."

"Do you want me to fuck you, Ivy?"

His face is expressionless, as if he is asking if I prefer regular or Diet Coke.

"Do you want to fuck me?" I volley back.

He grins maliciously. "When you saw me at my show in the enclosed room with Nyx on her knees, did it bother you?"

"If it did or didn't, it's none of my business."

Images of that night cloud my vision, squeezing my chest. I can't explain it.

" I told you. She didn't touch me, Ivy. I didn't fuck her, and she didn't suck my cock. Not since the first time I laid eyes on you."

"Why?"

"I think you know why."

I don't.

"I don't know why."

"Do you remember the first time you had a cock inside your pussy…do you remember what it felt like?"

I shake my head. "No. I can't remember what it felt like when he was…you know…inside me. All I remember was that he was small. It didn't hurt like I thought it would. I didn't come."

"How about Dean?"

"It was small, and I could never come. It felt fake… like… I was being filmed, and the walls were made from cardboard. I felt sick like was… doll in a costume."

"What did he make you wear?"

I look down at my boots for a second and then look up. "A pleated skirt…like a school uniform with the shirt."

His eyes gleam under the light of the moon like a feral animal.

"He was rough?"

I nod. "Yeah," I say softly.

"He paid you?"

"He knew I needed a ride home and the money. It didn't start like that at first, but then it…just was. I'm not…"

"A whore."

Two tears slide down my cheeks hearing that word out loud.

"I want to go home."

He walks to the driver's side door. "Then go home."

Confused, I step forward, and everything happens so fast. He starts the car. I go to open the passenger side door, but the door won't open. It's locked. I keep trying the handle, but it makes a *click, click* and won't budge.

I slap the window with the palm of my hand. "Draco, open the door!" I yell.

The car speeds off, kicking up dirt.

The cloud of dirt hits my eyes like tiny hot needles. The roar of the engine gets farther and farther as he drives off. Hot tears continue to slide down my dirt-stained cheeks.

He left me out here. He left me. He left me in the middle of nowhere, eight miles from home in the dark with no way to get home.

I panic.

"Draco!" I yell in a piercing scream. "Don't leave me! Please!"

My chest is rising and falling as I run toward the two red tail lights of his car. After I can't run anymore from exhaustion, my knees buckle and I fall, skinning my knees and ripping my black tights.

I pull out my phone from the side pocket of my jacket. No signal. I hold it up in the air getting up slowly, but nothing. Not even a bar on the screen.

He planned this.

But why?

None of it makes sense.

After walking for fifteen minutes, I see headlights coming in the opposite direction. Fear curls in my gut. I know not to flag a car down. No one good is out around midnight.

Panic sets in, firing my adrenaline. I run toward the tree line and hide.

The car slows down to a crawl. It's a van. My hands shake. It's dark, and I can't make out the van's color or see the license plate. I think whoever it is saw me because the van stops. I hear a door open.

I take off and run in the opposite direction.

A twig snaps in a subtle crack, shattering the stillness of the night. I freeze, my heart pounding as I try to hear any sign of someone following me. A chill sweeps through the trees. I don't know where I am or if I'm going in the right direction.

I move through the trees, my feet hitting the ground, rustling the leaves like drumbeats.

"Ivyyyyyyy!" I hear my name being called in a plaintive cry, followed by laughter in the distance.

"Ivyyyyy," my name is called again like a sigh in the wind. More laughter and then, "Don't leave me," the voice mocks.

My breath catches in my throat. The pulse in my veins quickens with every second. With every exhale I take, the cold air forms a wispy cloud before dissipating in the dark.

A loud snap from a twig to my right causes me to run.

Something long and hard grabs me around my waist, lifting me in the air.

"No!" I scream.

A large hand covers my mouth. I flail my arms and legs.

I'm slammed on the ground, knocking the wind out of me. I push with my hands and feet. I can't see who it is because it's so dark.

A hand grips my throat and squeezes, but I can still breathe. My tights are ripped to shreds. My skirt shoved above my waist.

"Please!" I plead on a cry.

"Scream my name!" My eyes go wide. " Say. My. Name." His tongue licks me like a dog. "Say it, my pretty little whore," he rasps against my cheek. "Scream my name!"

The grip on my throat relaxes. My body shakes uncontrollably from fear mixed with excitement.

Adrenaline and desire rush in my veins as his name escapes my lips followed by a cloud of smoke. "Draco."

He rips my shirt down the middle. My skirt follows and then my tights.

"Open your thighs, Ivy. I want to give you something you won't forget."

My thighs fall open, and the cold air kisses my heated clit.

Fuck.

I'm so fucking wet. I can come from just the cold breeze. I'm excited like in those porn movies when the man plays a game of cat and mouse with his prey.

His head dips between my legs. The flat part of his tongue swipes my slit.

I whimper at how my pulse pumps between my legs.

He growls, shoves his face between my legs like an animal and fucks me with his tongue.

"Mm," I groan. "Oh my God. Yes!"

His teeth nip at the soft skin of my inner thighs drawing blood. My clit matches the rapid pulse in my veins. I grip his hair and pull hard. I look down and watch as he eats me like an animal.

He lifts me up by gripping my ass and tongues my asshole. I push his face between my thighs, needing to come, but it's like he is in tune with my body and stops when I'm right at the edge.

He pulls away, and I feel a ghostly breeze from the wetness of his tongue. The sting from my knees and the small bites on my inner thighs.

I hear his zipper break through the silence. "Do you think I would leave you, Ivy?" he asks, pulling out his cock.

I can feel it in the inner side of my thighs. I look down as he rubs it where he bit me soothing the sting mixing it with blood. It glistens under the moon. It's huge with a big head and piercings down the underside of his shaft.

He presses the tip of his cock at the entrance of my pussy splitting it open. One hand is flat on the ground as he leans over me with placing his mouth near my ear. "I saw the sparkle in your eye when you realized it was me. The fear disappeared from your lungs. But I'm not a prince. I'm not a savior but I'm the man they all will fear if they so much as touch you. The only name screamed from your lips will be mine."

He strokes the top of his cock over my clit, and I can't take it. I come.

I grab his shoulders, we both watch as he holds the

head of his dick and flicks my clit as I come grinding my pussy over the head.

He strokes his cock, once, twice, and then, he groans.

Cum shoots like a jet, landing on the lips of my pussy, more coats my lower stomach.

When he's done, we are both panting. He brushes his lips over mine in a soft kiss and whispers, "I would never leave you."

CHAPTER TWENTY-TWO
DRACO

"FUN NIGHT?" Keir says in a hard tone when I walk inside the tent.

"Yes."

"Are you insane? If she tells anyone what you did, it could ruin us."

I smile wide. "I am considered"—I twirl my finger in circles over my temple—"a little loose upstairs if you know what I mean." I drop my smile. "She won't."

"How do you know that?"

I walk into our first-aid tent and grab the first-aid kit for her knees. I left her asleep in my bed. I need to bathe her and make sure her knees are tended to.

"Because I do."

He scoffs. "You think she's the one, don't you?" I grab the antiseptic and head back. But he blocks my path. "She isn't," he says, but I see it.

He wants her and I'm not sure in what way.

"You think by pulling a magic trick with a flower, she is going to kneel and suck your cock?"

"Don't do this, Draco. It's too much of a risk. You don't know for sure if she's the one."

She is. I feel it. I can see it in her eyes. She's mine,

and deep down, she feels it. Tonight proved more than I could have imagined. She's perfect.

"There is only one way to find out."

I step to the side, and he blocks me again. "I won't let you hurt her."

"That is not your call to make, and besides…" I lean close. "I've already painted her sweet pussy with my cum. If you touch her, I'll shove your teeth down your fucking throat and your magic fingers up your ass before I cut you open and watch you bleed." He pulls away, and I watch the fear burn in his eyes while I suck my lips dramatically. "I can still taste her on my tongue, Keir. Her fear is the fire in my crotch, and the taste of her cum is the scent on my skin. She's here."

"She won't let you kill me," he says hoarsely, but he's not convinced. I can see the doubt in his expression. He wants it to be her more than anything.

I chuckle. "Are you sure it's her?"

"It's her." I turn around, and Nyx walks in.

"You say that because he won't touch you since she showed up," Keir says.

I see the pained look in her expression. Keir wants to hurt her the same way I hurt him with the truth. I never meant to hurt her, and I told her that anything between us was transactional.

An act of pleasure and nothing more.

I could tell she doubted the day would ever come or that I would feel the need to end it. There was a time I thought it was all bullshit. That it wasn't real. The visions. Whatever tale my mother spilled was a crock of shit, but now that she is here, I believe it.

I believed it when I had my cock in my hand, and

Nyx was ready to suck it. It wasn't cooperating. I pictured my blond temptress, and all I saw was a woman who wasn't her. My cock had never malfunctioned before. I never thought it could happen. That was for fat men who were balding and hated what their life had become.

Nyx told me it happens but not to me. The way she looked seated in the audience and when she caught me with my pants down. I felt ashamed. I felt like I cheated on my girl. I was gutted and knew I had to do anything to get that image out of her mind.

"Nyx knows the rules and so do you,"I tell them and walk out.

I walk in my trailer and hear the shower running. I smile to myself and undress after placing the kit on the table.

I pull the door open, and the steam floats out like an exhaust pipe from the shower stall. Her body glistens under the spotlights. She swipes her hand to remove the fog from the glass. Her eyes dip to my hard cock, jutting out from between my legs. I'm so fucking hard and horny I think my cock will explode. I thought jerking off to her clit would take the edge off, but it has only made it worse.

"What are you doing?" she asks.

"The same thing you're doing, watching the show."

"I'm not a performer."

"You're my performer, and I'm the ringmaster. What I say goes unless you tell me no."

Her tits bounce when she swipes the glass again. "If I say no, it ends?"

"You have complete power over me. Except when I'm inside you."

"What do you mean?"

"Once you give me permission, I do what I want with your body. I fuck you how I want. How deep I want. How many times I want to come inside you. And make no mistake, Ivy, I will come inside you. I don't wear condoms size small."

She lowers her head to hide her grin. "Did you need something?"

"Yes, I need you."

"For?" I look down at my hard dick and then at her. "Oh…"

"Oh,"I mock. She pushes the glass door to the shower. "Is this you granting me permission?"

"Yes, but are you nice? Do you think you can be nice?"

"I can be whatever you want me to be when I'm with you, but you also have to let me do what I want."

"Which is?"

I walk inside the shower, the hot water hitting my skin. "Let me show you,"I say, pulling at my hard cock and stroking it while my balls hang tight.

I drop to my knees and lift her leg over my shoulder and shove my face into her cunt. She grinds her pussy, seeking my tongue. Her back is arched against the wall in the semi-darkness of the shower, and while I'm sucking her pussy, I fuck myself feeling my ribbed cock in my hand.

I look up, and the water streams down my neck and chest. My nose inhales her sweet scent as my tongue thrusts into her tight cunt, flicking it inside her.

Her tits glisten from the water. Her pink nipples beg for my teeth. I slide her leg off my shoulder and turn her around. I spread her perky ass cheeks and shove my tongue in her ass.

She moans from the pleasure while I slip two and then three fingers into her pussy. I tug on her clit, and she screams my name, urging me on.

"Draco," she moans. "More."

I smile and pump my tongue inside her ass until she comes.

After I shower and dry off, I tend to the scrapes on her knees with antiseptic and gauze. I dry her hair and comb the platinum strands like she's a delicate doll.

When I'm done, she smiles and grips my cock in her hand and sucks on the head, then glides her tongue over each piercing, flicking her tongue over each one.

"I'm fascinated by you," I tell her.

She smiles with my cock between her lips, and it's the greatest show on earth. The most important act in my life. Her fucking me.

I reach around her gorgeous ass, grateful for my height, and slide my finger into her pretty tight cunt. Then I bring my fingers to my mouth and suck on it, tasting the sweet saltiness of her pussy. "God, you are wet, Ivy. You are so fucking wet."

I pull her mouth off my cock and lay her back on the bed with her legs spread open. I push her lips apart so I can see how pink her cunt is inside. I grab my hard cock and stroke it, teasing her a bit. Her pussy clenches in want.

She pulls herself up by her elbows. Her nipples are hard, and her eyes beg me. They beg me to fuck her.

"Say it," I demand.

"Fuck me, Draco." She bucks her hips like she's possessed. "I want you to fuck me."

I move my mouth between her thighs and divide her body with my tongue, starting with the slit of her pussy to the valley of her chest. I suck her nipple and bite.

She lets out a loud moan, and her pussy leaks on my sheets. I do the same to the other, and more leaks, dripping to the crack of her ass. I glide my tongue down her stomach and lick her wet pussy, sucking it completely in my mouth.

Her fingernails dig in my scalp, and I groan from the pleasure of feeling her body tremble uncontrollably.

Ivy sits up, pulls her pussy away from my mouth, and kneels on the bed. Her lips are on my dick, and she takes it in her mouth as deep as she can go. She hesitates, and my balls are tight hitting her chin. I can tell by the way she hesitates and tries not to gag when the head of my cock touches the back of her throat with every thrust of my hips that it's her first time taking a man she wants.

I fist her hair in both hands like the strands are makeshift handles and fuck her mouth.

She gasps for air, but I hold her steady until her throat relaxes and then keep fucking her mouth until my cock is buried deep and her mouth is near the base of my cock.

I look down and her top lip rubs against the stubble of shaved pubic hair.

"You're fucking amazing," I praise. "Such a dirty girl." I lean close, causing my cock to slip out of her mouth coated with saliva. "You're my whore, Ivy. My pretty whore." Her eyes flash with saliva dripping down her chin.

She hates that word, but I'll teach her to like it.

Her hands rub over the hard muscles of my abs. Her fingers trace every dip of muscle to the valley that makes up the v that runs down my hips. I push her back on the bed and hold her legs as wide as they can go, digging my thumbs in her inner thighs. I surprise her when I release them and lick the drool from her chin and kiss her deeply on the lips.

My fingers push the strands of hair away from her forehead and look deep in her eyes. My hard cock, desperate to cum, presses between her legs.

"Ivy?"

"Yeah?"she says breathlessly and almost whimsical.

"I'm going to take you how I want now. Is that okay?"

"Will you hurt me?"

"Have I?"

"No, but will you?"

I give her a wicked smile. "There's only one way to find out."

I slide into her with one powerful thrust, causing her back to arch.

The rest happens in slow motion.

The air escapes her lungs. My nostrils flare from the pleasure of her tight cunt gripping my ribbed cock. I don't move so I don't tear her and give her time to adjust to my size.

Her hands grip my arms and slide to my ass, holding me inside her.

She gasps for air. "Draco?"

Her face is a mixture of pleasure and pain.

"I won't move. I'm waiting for you. I will never hurt you unless you like it."

"I'm afraid to move,"she says.

"Play with your clit."

Her dainty fingers find where we are joined.

It's pure.

Raw.

She strums her clit, and her inner walls choke my cock. I grind my hips, pushing deep and slow. She meets my slow, measured thrusts. I suck her nipples, squeezing her full breasts gently like two ripe fruits.

I lift one leg over my arm, place my hand flat on the headboard, and fuck her. The slapping sound of skin adds to the pounding beat of my heart.

"Draco,"she pleads. "Don't stop. I'm…coming."

I continue to fuck her hard. Her tits bounce with each thrust. I'm in heaven burning from the fire of hell from being this long without her. My balls tighten, and I come hard inside her cunt. A loud groan mixes with her sweet cries as I break her apart over and over.

When we are done, I look down at my cock buried in her tight pink cunt. I stare at the thin strip of hair on her pussy and grin.

I look up after releasing her leg. "You're a blond."

She points at her hair, messy from fucking. "I am."

"You're a real blonde,"I add.

Her cheeks flush bright red. "Oh."

"I like it."

There is nothing about her I don't like. I hope she feels the same way when she finds out who I really am.

CHAPTER TWENTY-THREE

I SQUINT from the sun streaming through the window, and for a second, I think I'm in my room. Yet it doesn't smell like stale cigarettes mixed with pine cleaner but of citrus and cedar.

I have a pleasant ache between my thighs from being fucked all night. He didn't stop until I passed out from exhaustion. I didn't think one could pass out from coming so much.

The door opens, and I smile, but it fades when I see that it's Nyx. It's not that I hate her or anything, but I was hoping it was Draco. I take that back. I'm jealous of how effortlessly gorgeous she looks with her makeup on. Her eyes are lined with red and a smoky eye that looks hot. Her lips are blood red. She is always dressed and ready to perform. Her skin is white with a hint of pink. She wears a shiny black bodysuit with garters, ripped tights, and laced black heeled boots. Her hair is grayish-white with dark roots, and I love the color of her eyes. They are a mix between violet and blue.

"Good afternoon,"she says with a salacious smile.

"Shit." I reach for my phone, and it's 1 p.m. I have to get ready for my shift soon, and I promised Alice we would hang out. "I have to get ready for work soon."

She angles her head. "Work?"

"Yeah."

I slide off the bed and look at my knees and smile. He bandaged them and put a Band-Aid on with clown faces like I'm five. His black T-shirt hits right above my knees. I look around for my clothes but don't see them anywhere.

She pouts. "You got hurt."She shakes her head slowly. "You can't go to work if you're hurt." She places a finger on her lip. "Draco…" She looks up. "You don't need to work. You can stay here with us."

I walk into the bathroom and find a brand-new electric toothbrush with little clowns on it that says PUSH ME I SPIN.

I pick it up and find it hot that he left it for me.

After I freshen up, I walk out and find Nyx watching me.

I raise my brows with a smirk. "Had fun?"

"Oh… I'm just getting started. I want to suck your pussy."

Well, at least she's honest. I've never had a girl eat me out before. I can't say I have never thought of it or wanted to try it, but it's been in the back of my mind when I think about sex.

The times I've had sex with Dean and the first time with Tommy had me questioning my sexuality at one point. I never liked it, but Draco solidified that I like men. But I wouldn't deny the opportunity to try something new. To explore. In a safe way.

"What would Draco think?"

I wonder if this was a one-time thing. I knew what to expect sleeping with him. I fantasized about having sex with him since I met him, and he touched me for the first time.

When they both said there was nothing serious between them, how could I refuse? He's dangerously hot, and I want him more than I have ever wanted anything in my whole life. The fact that he's the ringleader in a circus makes me want him even more. He says he isn't a prince, but to me, he's more than a prince. To me, he's every dream come true.

"He would watch if you let me. If you say yes of course." She stands, placing a hand on her hip and angles her head to the side. "You must be sore. You two were fucking the whole night." Her eyes dip to my hard nipples protruding from his T-shirt. "I was jealous." My chest squeezes. "Not because of him," she says coyly. "Because I wanted to taste you, Ivy. I was jealous he made you come, and I wasn't there to lick it from your cunt."

The way she says lick and cunt has my poor pussy throbbing.

"I-I…"

"Have you ever let a girl fuck you with her tongue?"

"No."

Her eyes turn a shade of dark purple. Her fingers play with the hem of my T-shirt. "Can I dress you up so we can play? This is a circus after all," she adds. "I promise to make you… pretty. Sexy. Draco will jerk off all night when they see what I've done with you."

"Draco?" I ask confused.

"Oops," she says, laughing dramatically. "Did I say that?"

"You did."

She giggles like a little girl. "Draco is craaaazy about you. He can't stop staring at you or talking about you. He warned everyone."

"About what?"

"How he will kill anyone who touches you."

"Why?"

She squeals. "Because silly, you're his woman. The one he's been waiting for and…now you're here, and we should play." She slides clown slippers from the corner of the bed toward me with her boot. I put them on, and she pulls me by the arm out of the trailer. "You'll look amazing in this outfit,"she rambles on. "By the way, your tits look amazing."

I STARE at myself in front of the mirror in the dressing tent. She made me into an erotic female ringleader with leather boots over netted tights, my ass hanging out of short black shorts with a bra that has little gold buttons and coins hanging along the edge by the swell of my breasts. It's practically a bathing suit.

My hair is straight, and my makeup is done up like hers, but with more detail and more black smoke around my eyes, plus little jewels stuck to my skin. My lips are painted black with red lip liner. I look like I'm going to a Halloween party at a strip club called Siren Seduction.

"So what do you think?" She leans over my shoulder behind me with her red lips close to my ear. I stare at myself in the mirror. "I think you look hot." Her hand cups me between my legs. "You feel hot too, Ivy." Her breath fans the painted skin on my neck. "Let's give them a show, baby. A special show." I turn my head. "Freaks only,"she says with her lips brushing mine. Her eyes promise me relief from the soreness between my legs.

I follow her to the clear box made of acrylic. I thought it was glass at first, but it isn't. It's huge when I follow her inside and looking out from within. It's big and feels like a room on the set of the movie *The Truman Show* where everyone who wants to watch gets a glimpse of your life.

I stand in front of a leather chaise with chains attached underneath. She motions for me to kneel on all fours with my ass sticking straight up in the air.

"You are so swollen. He's been fucking you hard all night." My pussy is swollen and engorged. I can feel the heat from the cool air hitting my battered cunt. "You have a pretty pussy, Ivy. I can't blame him for fucking you the way he did."

Awareness snakes up my spine. I look over my shoulder, and he's watching like a spectator with no shirt and black pants. He slams his hand on the hard acrylic. His eyes are riveted on my pussy when she spreads my ass cheeks open.

"Nyx,"he warns.

"She needs to be taken care of, Draco. You can't leave her in bed to go train. You don't know what might come crawling in to take a bite," she says with a laugh.

Nyx is a little crazy, but I like her.

"Nyx,"he warns again in a hard tone.

"Just a little taste. She wants it, Draco. Doesn't she look spectacular?" She blows on my pussy. "So soft and

delicate. You know how I feel about women—about her."
I look over my shoulder. My eyes find hers. "I want you
more than I want him, Ivy. He knew what would happen
when he found you. I know it all sounds a bit crazy," she
says in a childlike voice. "But we're all under your spell.
Show him how gorgeous you are, Ivy. Show him why he
shouldn't ever leave you alone," she says slowly.

My pussy is heavy and soaked. Draco walks in and
lifts my chin delicately with one finger, careful not to ruin
my makeup, and says with a thick British accent, "Welcome to the Circle of Freaks, my love. I own you now."
He looks up. "Suck her pussy, Nyx." He leans close when
my body jerks forward from the pleasure of her tongue
and whispers, "Don't get used to this, Ivy. I turn
murderous when someone else touches what is mine."

I bite my inner cheek when her mouth sucks my cunt,
stifling a moan.

"Does that go for you too?" I ask between breaths.

I don't know why I said that. I don't know what is
happening to me. Everything is happening so fast.

He sticks his thumb in my mouth. "You're the only
woman who will touch me, and I'm the only man who
will touch you. This is to appease your curiosity." Nyx
tongues my pussy and then fucks me. I push against her
face. She groans. Her mouth feels amazing. I'm about to
come. I suck his thumb and moan.

I cry out when she takes her tongue out and glides
the tip in my ass.

I pull my mouth from his thumb and moan.

My inner thighs are slick.

"Draco," I plead.

Nyx lets out a crazy laugh. "Mm…poor baby."

I need to come. She's fucking torturing me.

"Fun is over, Nyx."

She kisses my pussy. "I'm sorry," she says in a naughty little voice.

"Go," he demands.

She walks around and tilts my head, then kisses me on my lips. "You're so beautiful," she says and licks my lips and whispers. "He's jealous, and I don't blame him."

Draco doesn't wait for her to leave the room before he spreads my sore pussy with his fingers. I feel something wet that feels like lube, and then he slides his cock slowly in.

I moan on her lips. He pushed deeper.

I close my eyes. "Mm…"

"You like his fat pierced cock inside you…don't you, Ivy?"

I nod, and she drowns out the moan escaping my lips with her mouth when his piercing hits the right spot.

Draco fucks me while she deepens the kiss. My arms shake on the chaise. My pussy makes sucking noises with every thrust. Draco's fingers dig in my hips as he picks up speed.

Little gasps escape my throat, and it's like Nyx and I are breathing the same air. Her tongue licks the roof of my mouth. Her red lipstick smears like blood is dripping down her chin.

I tilt my head back when my orgasm slams into me. Our tongues tangle while she pinches my nipples.

I let out a scream when my orgasm peaks. It feels so fucking good.

I feel alive.

"I'm coming," Draco growls. "Fuck!" He slams into

me, gripping my ass in his hands at the same time as he pulls me hard against him with a loud smack. His cock convulses in my pussy followed by the heat of his cum.

Nyx breaks the kiss and says, "You are perfect for him."

CHAPTER TWENTY-FOUR

AFTER NYX TOUCHES up my makeup, she smiles. "It's time."

"Time for what?"

"To show you, silly." Her smile widens. "It's showtime."

She has a disturbed look in her eyes. I'm not going to like whatever she is going to show me or rather they are going to show me, but I want to know. I've seen fucked-up things in my life. Things no girl should see but had to accept because there was no other choice. Things I've had to do because it was what my mother said I was destined for.

Nyx takes me to another tent, and it smells like formaldehyde. The same smell the first time I saw the fake body parts in the pickled jars.

We walk through the exhibit with red lights that shine on a shelf with a row of jars. One has eyes, a spine, what looks like a pair of lungs, and another jar with a tongue. That jar reads LIAR in big glowing letters.

"They look so real," I say distractedly.

She laughs and then stops dramatically. "That's because they are."

"W-what?" I stammer. She's fucking with me, but the

way she looks at the jars and then at me tells me she isn't.
"N-no. You're joking."

I jolt when a large hand lands on my shoulder. I look
up. "You scared me."

"It's what we do here,"Draco says in a calm voice.

He takes my hand and tugs me deeper inside the tent.
There is a large box the size of a shipping container with
what looks like soundproofing on the sides. It's dark the
farther we walk inside. The door slams shut behind us,
and I panic.

I whirl around, but Draco grips my shoulders turning
me back. "Shh…"

"It's okay, baby," Nyx coos. "You'll get used to it."

Who the fuck are these people? I blink. My eyes sting
from the smell. It smells like copper.

A light shines from above, and then there are muffled
screams.

I turn around and almost gag from the bile that rises
from my throat. Five men are tied to metal chairs gagged
and bloody.

The rest of the performers stand behind them. Lex
with an ax. Keir with a chainsaw. The Butcher with a
butcher knife dressed like they're going to begin a show.
But this is a different show. One man has been mutilated.
Blood is splattered everywhere. He is missing his limbs.
His guts are spilling out of his stomach.

I throw up, not being able to take it. I retch until
nothing comes out. "What the fuck?"I back away toward
the exit, but Draco blocks my path. "Why?"

"Let us explain,"Draco says. He points at the others,
who look like they are an inch away from dying. "They
rape and kill girls, Ivy." He steps closer, towering over me.

"It's why they can't find who is doing it. There are more." He tilts his head. "So many. They are like a disease that has infected our society. Poisoning the girls who never survive. Their souls scream in pain from the innocence that was taken. They need to be eradicated, not placed in jail so that they have a chance to breathe."

I shake my head. "How do you know?"

"I was one of them." Nyx steps forward. "Draco saved me." She looks behind me. "The Circle of Freaks saved me. They are not just a circus. They are my saviors. I love them. They gave me a home. You see, I don't have parents. The guys who took me killed them and trafficked me from Russia when I was twelve. I was raised by the circus, Ivy. It's all I know. They gave me a home. A place. A new identity."

My chest squeezes. Twelve? I shake my head. I need to get out of here. It's too much. I can't…

"I want to leave. I have work," I say and step around him toward the exit.

CHAPTER TWENTY-FIVE

I WATCH Alice sleeping on my bed. I tried after school, work, and then the bar. I couldn't tell her about Draco or the Circle of Freaks and what I saw. Draco told me not to tell anyone about us and that soon he would come for me.

Whatever that meant.

He forgot to mention that they kill the men raping and killing the girls. They obviously couldn't find the girls after they find out who did it or which one they abducted. I'm sure they get them to talk when they mutilated them.

After he dropped me off at work, I assured him I had a ride home. I could tell by his facial expression he wasn't happy when I asked to leave or the way he drover off when I got out of his car without a backward glance.

There was so much I wanted to ask. So much I didn't know.

My mother called me repeatedly, asking me if I had the rent money. I was worried she would kick me out.

Where would I go? The circus? Be part of their murder crew?

I had to finish school. I had to forget what I saw, but I knew something like that wasn't so simple.

To some, they would be considered them no different from the men who abducted and killed those girls. They had a point about them going to jail and it bot being fair when those girl's lives had been cut short in the worst way.

The authorities would do the same if they caught them and obviously couldn't stop it from happening again. Who would catch the rest? Those men would be set free eventually, and the cycle would continue. It won't change that those girls are dead. The Circle of Freaks didn't kill them, or did they?

I watch Alice while I get dressed for school. The memory from last night in her room floods back. After everything I saw, I needed to feel normal. I didn't want her to feel what I was feeling. I wanted to her to feel wanted. Sexy. Loved.

We all have secrets. I could see that she had them in her eyes last night, and I wanted to do something I never had the courage to do with Nyx. I wanted to taste a woman's pussy. I never expected Alice to be so responsive. So sexy.

It was a one-time thing.

In a way, I felt I was cheating on Draco, but deep down, I knew I wasn't. If he was in the room, he would watch. He would make sure I was able to come.

I push her on the bed after sucking her mouth and tits. I remove my clothes and pull her panties off until we are both naked on her bed. Her pussy is wet and glistening from the light on her nightstand.

I play with my pussy, and Alice watches me masturbate with three fingers. I play with my clit and then take my fingers and slide them past her lips, and she sucks them, tasting me.

She opens her legs. Her pussy is clean and pink. She spreads her lips with her fingers. Her clit is swollen and a shade darker. I press my face into her pussy, licking and sucking her clit. She tastes sweet.

Her fingers slide in my hair, massaging my head while she arches her back, and I make her come. She bites the edge of her pillow to stifle her moans. Her pussy is dripping from her cum, and I suck her clean.

I wipe my mouth with the back of my hand. She faces me, kneeling in the same position on the bed. She dips her head and sucks my tits while sliding a finger in my pussy. Another finger works my clit. I look down and watch her tongue licking my nipple and then the other.

"Alice," I hiss from the pleasure of her tongue and fingers.

She pushes me onto the bed so that my head is toward the head-board and dips her face between my legs and sucks my pussy. I grind my hips, feeling her tongue inside me. She moans and caresses my outer thighs. I play with my tits while my orgasm slams into me. Her tongue continues to flick my clit.

When I think we are done, Alice surprises me by lying on top of me. She kisses me, grinding on my pussy like she has a cock. She cups my face and continues to kiss me with a smile.

She pulls away and lies over me in a sixty-nine position and I eat her pussy. She spreads my legs and eats me out. We fuck each other with our tongues. I spread her ass and suck her clit, then lick her asshole. She likes it because she grinds her pussy on my face, and I slide my tongue in her pussy and fuck her.

She pushes my legs wider and slides her tongue in my ass then sucks my clit. We are both moaning, fucking each other with our tongues until we both come ate the same time.

When we are done, we snuggle in each other's arms and before we fall asleep, we say, "This is our secret," at the same time.

I laugh. "It was a one-time thing, Alice."

"I love you, Ivy," she says and falls asleep.

"I love you too, Alice," I whisper and kiss her temple.

I look at the bedroom door and see the shadow of footsteps retreating. I know he was listening. Fear curls around my heart. Her stepfather is a creep. I know guys like him and what they do.

I have to protect Alice.

AFTER ALICE TOOK me to school, I thought the reporters would have been gone by the time school was out but they are everywhere.

On the sidewalk, parking lot, and bus lane. Mich and his friends were killed last night and mutilated. Body parts were missing. Based on the media reports, eyes, tongues, and their penis were removed. It is big news compared to months of girls gone missing and later found dead.

Unknown: Are you afraid?

Ivy: Of what, the big bad wolf?

I'm standing on the sidewalk, watching the solemn look on girls who knew Mich. It sucks that a group of people died, but some people don't deserve to live if they do things that make people wish they were dead.

Unknown: Aren't you going to ask me?

Ivy: Ask you what?

The first school bus drives off. I rush over to the last one but freeze. The blacked-out Cuda is idling on the curb across the street.

Unknown: Come with me and find out. I'm sure I have something you want.

Ivy: Cocky.

Unknown: It's aching, baby.

I smile, but it dies when Tommy walks up. "Hey, Ivy."

"What do you want? I gotta go."

"In a rush?" he says, staring at my chest.

"Yes."

He grabs my wrist when I take a step to go around him.

"Is there a problem?"

I look behind Tommy as he slowly turns around. "Who the fuck are you?" Tommy says, looking up at Draco.

"Name a place you'll never see your name," Draco replies.

Tommy squares off but doesn't release the grip on my wrist. I can feel the waves of testosterone flying between them. Draco's gaze dips to Tommy's hand on my wrist.

Tommy smiles. "You think you're funny. Dressed all in black. You look like a wannabe singer in a band from your mother's basement." Tommy lowers his voice. "Did she tell you I was her first? That I fucked her."

"Yes, we talk about it. She told me all three minutes of it. Kinda boring and lame if you ask me." Draco lowers his voice. "But don't worry. Your secret is safe with me. It's okay to have a small dick. She likes mine so much better." He resumes his normal tone. "Back to naming a place. Answer, and if you get it wrong, I'll tell you. It will be a glimpse of your future. I'll be nice and give you a hint. It's a special place."

Tommy looks between us, confused. He isn't sure if Draco is pissed off or not, or crazy.

"I don't know, man," he says, defeated.

"A gravestone."

I finally pull my wrist free when it takes Tommy a minute to let the answer sink in.

"Are you threatening me?" Tommy asks spitefully.

"How can I threaten you with death when we are all meant to die?"

"You're fucking crazy, man."

"We are all crazy about something."

Draco grabs my hand and caresses the spot where Tommy grabbed my wrist like he's erasing his touch from my skin.

Once we are in his car, I look out the window to see Tommy staring at Draco's car as we drive off.

"Are you going to kill him?" I ask.

"What would you like me to do?"

I snort. "If you can get him to stop calling me a slut around school, that would be great. Slut and my name go hand in hand these days."

"I'm sorry."

"For?"

"For what I said. For what I asked. It was…out of line."

"I can't change what anyone thinks of me. I've learned that since I was a little girl. The show must go on, right? I'm just the act."

"Is that what you think of me?"

"If it wasn't… you wouldn't have said it," I say honestly. After a few seconds of silence. I clear my throat, changing the subject. "Thanks for picking me up from school. You didn't have to do that."

He doesn't answer and stares straight ahead. I shouldn't have said that, but it's the truth. I got used to people judging me.

When I was eleven, my mother told me not to cry over spilled milk. I tried to change what people thought of me, but when I couldn't, I learned to accept and stop running from it.

He slows down by the Big H but keeps going.

"You missed the plaza," I tell him.

"I know."

"I can't be late to my shift."

I need Alice to pick me up so I can keep a close eye on her.

"I don't like you working there."

"I don't either, but I have bills to pay."

"Like?"

"Rent, my phone, the light?"

"Your mom?"

"Says she doesn't make enough."

"She's a liar."

"I don't have a choice, Draco."

"We all have a choice."

"What is the real reason?"

"Alice. She's…"

"My brother is taking care of it."

"Your brother?"

He pulls through the gate behind the haunted carnival. Drives around the back near is trailer and places the car in park.

Who's his brother? Then, it slowly dawns.

Lazarus.

"Lazarus is my brother, Ivy. We own"—he waves his hand toward the fair— "all this and more."

"I'm confused? Does Alice know? She's in trouble, Draco. She will be coming to pick me up from work."

Panic sets in. They've been watching us. Alice. Me. The ticket. It was all deliberate.

He turns in his seat and faces me. "Ivy?"

"You're scaring me."

"Don't be afraid. The house. It brought you to me."

"The house?"

A flashback of the house. Me and Alice. The fortune teller Seraphina.

I shake my head, not believing. The killings. The manor. Alice saying her car is charged every morning. The jars. The same ones with the body parts inside them at their exhibit. The old lady buying them every week at the grocery store.

"No."

"The circus calls to you, Ivy, because in another life, you were part of a circus. This circus. With me."

I shake my head in denial. "You're lying. I'm not…"

"You were my wife and will be my wife in this life and the next. Your connection to Alice is strong because she

lived in that house with you in another life. The house…
brings you back in every life for eternity. Our love is
eternal in this life and the next. You will have a son, and
Alice will have two. In this life, the way things turn out
will depend on certain aspects of free will and…the way
the house wants it to be. You will have visions and so will
Alice when the time comes. The house will guide you
both."

My hands tremble in my lap. "You're crazy. You're
going to kill me."

"I'm not, but I will kill whoever touches you."

"I fucked Alice," I confess.

He smiles. "Pity, I wasn't there to watch. My brother
will be so disappointed."

"You're not mad?"

"No. If that is what you both wanted. You have a gift,
my love. I don't think there is anyone who could resist
you. It is *your* gift and I've been waiting for you."

Something doesn't add up. How?

"If this is a gift, then there is a curse, right? There is
always a curse."

"We die together. So will Alice and Lazarus. We die
young, Ivy. After death, we reincarnate in another life. It
is different every time. Our souls are all linked. The
house will call us back, but the circus goes on." He
caresses my lips with the pad of his thumb. "It will come
to you, Ivy. Don't fight it. Our love will come to you. I'll
come to you in your dreams, and I will be the nightmare
to those who have wronged you. It is all tied to you."

A chill runs up my thighs. "I'm scared. I don't want
to die."

"You're not really dead and you don't really die. You

want to be part of a circus? Then let me show you. My mother… she wasn't wrong about you."

"What did she say?" I ask curiously.

"She said when I saw my love again, I would fall in love at first sight." His eyes trail over my face. "And she was right. I'm in love with Ivy Sloan, and my biggest fear is the day she stops loving me back."

He gets out of the car, leaving me staring straight ahead.

After two or three minutes, I hear a tap on my window.

I open the door with a smile.

"Keir."

"At your service," he announces with a bow.

I step out and take in his performer's outfit. He's wearing a black and red medieval frock coat over tight leather pants. His chest is smooth and chiseled.

"You must have all the ladies in the audience going crazy."

"As much as I try to impress the audience, I haven't found the one who would give me her heart."

"I'm sure she will be very special. Whoever she is."

"I hope to find her one day."

"You will."

I turn and see Lex and her gorgeous fire-engine-red hair.

"Hi, I'm Lex. Remember me?"

"I could never forget you. You both look gorgeous and spectacular."

"I was hoping you would want to rehearse with us. We would love to have you in our next show."

"Oh," I say with disbelief. "I have no experience. Where would I..."

"It will come back to you," Keir says like we share a special secret. A special bond and I'm supposed to remember.

I'M ON STAGE, and to my left, a curtain rolls up. Draco stands shirtless with black pants and his face painted with black-and-white face paint. I look at my outfit, hoping I look okay. Nyx applied my makeup, and I'm wearing the same outfit I wore Friday night.

"Ready?"

"I'm not sure what you expect me to do. I can't do" —I point at Nyx flying in the air by her hair—"that."

"You're a seductress. You can captivate anyone. All you have to do is walk on the stage and be you. It is in your soul, Ivy. Let it out. Show me what you want."

I want him, but I don't tell him that.

"Later, we have business to take care of. We are not trying to hide anything from you," the Butcher says. "You were the one who started it all, Ivy. We all come back because of you."

I look at Keir, and his eyes are transfixed on me. How could I have started it all? What does he mean?

"Saving the girls," Keir says, quieting my thoughts. "Girls being abducted and trafficked has been going on for centuries. The 1800s and before that. You and..."

I look at Draco. "It's true," Draco says. "We became

a traveling circus because of you. You wanted to find the girls who went missing and hurt the ones responsible. You lured…"

The men. The old me from the past seduced the men who were sick. The ones I knew would rape or had raped and hurt young girls.

"There is a difference between consent and…" Lex pauses. "Nonconsensual sex and being a sick animal."

"Women are beautiful. They should be respected and set free. We…" Nyx stops and lowers herself from the harness. "We are free because of your family. You, Draco, L, and his love."

They don't know about Alice yet. L stands for Lazarus. I have been trying to piece everything together. The signs.

"Stop thinking so much about everything," Draco says, walking up behind me. I can feel his hard cock on my lower back. "Let go, Ivy. Show me your soul."

His voice echoes in my head. I close my eyes, and a flash back to a different time comes into focus.

A woman with a long robe sways her hips while walking on stage.

She removes the robe, and her lips are the shade of bright blood. Her hair is ghostly white. Glitter all over her skin with red sequins on her shorts. There is a crowd in the distant background.

She looks over her shoulder. "Are you ready for me?" she says playfully. She tilts her head back and laughs. "I love you, Draco." Her voice repeats like a ritual.

"You're so gorgeous they are going to love you, Mrs. Hades," the man says. I try to look at his face, but all I can make out is the top hat. The ringmaster.

I jolt, gasping for air. "Ivy!" My shoulders shake. I'm

out of breath, my lungs starved of oxygen. "Ivy, are you alright?" Keir asks with a worried expression.

My chest is rising and falling. I nod, trying to swallow.

"Yes," I say, taking another breath. "Hades?"

"Draco Hades."

"Hade's manor?"

The rest of the performers arrive, and everyone goes to the back of the stage to rehearse.

"Yes. It's our family estate. I believe Alice lives there with her mother. Her father is missing at the moment. I don't think he intends to return," Draco says.

He's dead because I told him about Alice. But if he is a Hades, then his brother already knew about him. Lazarus has been watching for Alice. But for how long?

"Where do I fit in all this?"

"Here with me. There is no reason for you to work at the Big H. You'll be taken care of."

"School?"

"By the time we hit the road, you should have graduated. I don't intend to take you until you finish school and we have handled our little problem."

He means the men killing girls.

"You have…"

"What we need. Don't worry, Ivy. I don't intend to stop eating pussy at thirty-five and start collecting two-dollar bills. I don't think we will last that long. "

"You've thought of everything."

"You had a vision, didn't you?"

Is that what that was?

"Yes," I admit.

"The more we are around each other, the more you

will have them. It is of all the past lives we have shared. You've always had them since it started."

"How..."

"You will know...in time." He holds out his hand. "I have a surprise for you, but right now, we need to practice. The show must go on, and I'm DYING to be seduced."

CHAPTER TWENTY-SIX

AT SCHOOL THE NEXT DAY, I watch as people walk out of the main building laughing and shaking their heads. I'm curious about why I keep getting weird glances, but then I see it.

All over the walls and lockers is my surprise. Posters of Tommy strapped to a chair buck naked with a close-up of his small penis with a large arrow pointed at it all over the school.

In big letters, it reads:

TOMMY HILL HAS A SMALL DICK.

"Holy shit," I whisper with a smile.

When I make it to my locker, I see Tommy trying to pull the posters off the walls, but they fly like leaves all over the floor.

Girls giggle, and guys point at the posters, cackling in laughter.

Principal Miller storms out of the front office, yelling, "Who did this! When I catch the ones responsible, they will be arrested." He pauses when he sees me. "Did you have anything to do with this?"

Anger bubbles in my veins at the accusation. "I don't

know, Mr. Miller. I think you should worry about the girls who keep popping up missing. I don't see you distraught over it, but when pictures pop up all over the school of a quarterback who likes to fuck half the school, you seem a little bothered by it." I shake my head in disappointment. "Not a good look, Miller."

"Watch your tone with me, young lady."

"Be careful, Mr. Miller, I'm an adult. I could report you to the school board on how you treat young girls unfairly." I lean close. "How excited you get when you talk to them alone in your office."

His face drains of all color, and then he storms off.

I hear a locker door close and look up. "Alice," I call out.

She smiles. "I have an idea."

"Do you?" I tease.

She gives me a look that says, *I know as much as you.* But does she?

AFTER SCHOOL, Draco picks me up, ignoring Jason's stare and Tommy's sneer as I walk out to the car. I don't tell Draco the bad feeling I have in the pit of my stomach about Jason but I don't want tell because I don't want to sour the him.

"Where are we going?" I ask.

"Home."

"The circus?"

"No, our home."

He pulls up to the manor, and now it feels familiar. Not like when I've picked up Alice or the last time I was in her room. I squeeze my legs together at the memory. I notice Alice is not home yet. I look over at Draco when he drives around to the side of the house where there is a black metal gate and a door with a knocker with a metal iron mask like the ones you see in medieval times.

When he opens the door, it's part of the house that mirrors where Alice stays. It feels like I've been here before. It smells of citrus and cedar.

"It smells like…"

"Citrus and cedar," he finishes for me.

"How did you…?"

"It's always been your favorite."

I walk into the kitchen, and it looks just like the main house. The staircase. The hallways.

"Is this the same…?"

"It's the same house, but the only access is through a hidden door by the piano. When you walk through, you will be right in the living room like a mirage."

"But you can't see it from the main house."

"The first Hades brother designed it that way when the prophecy began and his brother was born."

"Who started…?"

He turns around. "You did."

"How?"

"I can't tell you that."

"Why?"

"It hurts too much."

"If you care about me and want me to believe all this is real. Why…?"

"You had a daughter. *We*…had a daughter once. She

was your second born. The first generation of Hades children. I'm older and so are you compared to Lazarus and Alice."

I walk over to the books on the shelves. Compared to the other side these shelves are full and those are empty. I place my index finger over the spines and notice there are first editions.

"What happened?"

He lowers his head like he is pained to tell me. "She was taken," he says softly.

My heart drops, and my hands start to tremble. "Taken?"

He cups my cheek. "It drove you to madness. You…It drove me to protect you. To protect this family and everyone you loved." His eyes hold mine for a second. "Performing is what got us through it, and…"

"Trying to save the others from it happening again."

He holds me in his arms. "Yeah."

A wave of dizziness hits me. I close my eyes and hear a little girl's laughter. She's maybe eleven or twelve. *"I'm right here, Momma,"* she says playfully, waving at me from the old small Ferris wheel. She throws her head back laughing, and then the image fades away.

A sob escapes my throat. My knees buckle. His strong arms keep me from falling. A pain slices into me so deep. So big, it rips right through me.

"I got you, Ivy," he rasps against my temple. "I have you, baby."

"I saw her," I cry out. "I saw her, Draco."

"I know."

"I'm sorry. It's why I didn't want to tell you." He

steadies me. "It brings her back but it also brings the pain."

"I want it. All of it, and don't do that to me again."

I watch his throat work. "I'm sorry."

"Take me back."

He knows I mean to the circus. I want to go back.

I WALK IN THE TENT. Nyx gives me a wide, crazy smile.

"Get me ready," I tell her.

"With pleasure," she says and then giggles madly.

After I'm in costume, I walk out the same side the night Draco took me to get something to eat with Bozo and find Madam Seraphina's booth.

The sun has almost completely set by the time I knock on the wood that says Psychic Readings. FREAK ACCIDENTS DO HAPPEN. SEE ALL KNOW ALL.

"Yes," she calls out.

I walk inside, and when she looks up from rummaging with something from her trunk as she gets dressed before the park opens. Her eyes widen.

"Mrs. H…Ivy Sloan."

"You said I would have dreams, not visions."

She waves her hand. "Dreams. Visions. Same thing."

"So it is true."

"Yes."

"How do you fit in all this?"

"You brought my family here from Europe. Italy, to be precise. Generations of my family are psychics."

"Can you find the girls?"

She gives me a wan smile. "That is like asking me for the winning lottery numbers. If I did know them, I wouldn't be here, and the answer is no. You asked centuries ago the same question, and the answer is still *no*. I'm sorry."

I take a seat and watch her wrap her shawl around her neck.

The gold coins clink when she adjusts it as she settles in her chair.

"It's not your fault. Did we ever…?"

"No. She was never found. My mother warned me you would ask this question as my grandmother and hers before her. They all said the same thing when you asked."

"My son."

"Was one of the best performers and he married his love. The twin soul you and his brother's love carry inside your hearts will split when it is time. It's quite fascinating, I assure you. Your child's love and soul stays dormant in the mother, keeping pure love alive until it's time and you pass . That twin soul reincarnates in another female, keeping your family's legacy alive. When you give birth to your son and your sister-in-law does the same, you dream of how they meet their soul mate so you can prepare your sons for their true love when they find each other. The house."

"What about it?"

"It is the key. It brings you all together. It heals. It destroys all who want to harm you. It is the pact you made with the house and the one you made the pact with."

"With whom?"

"He shall not be named. He is not the God that you pray to or the devil. He breathes in the wind. The keeper of the forest. The tarot guided you. You wanted to be immortal in away. Live young, die young and in return you reincarnate but you had to sacrifice. The loss of your daughter was too great. The love in your heart for Draco greater."

A little girl's voice whispers, "Cernunnos."

"Cernunnos."

She smiles. "She told you. The voice you hear is your daughter. Cernunnos has her. He gave you a way to rebirth and a way to regenerate your bloodline. He is part man. Part stag." She rubs the crystal ball on her table. "In return, you and Draco swore to never use animals out of respect. The lord of wild things granted you a gift. His lover and wife is the goddess of spring, Beltane. Goddess of fertility, which means…"

"We all give birth and die together, but we keep going."

"Sexuality of life and earth. Your husband is eccentric. He is the joker, one might say."

"Did my husband ever love another?"

I don't know why I asked. Maybe because of Nyx and the past.

"Once you meet, he can't. The bond and love is… too great."

"But I…"

"Sucked pussy and had yours sucked?"

I look up, shocked that she would say it aloud. How did she…?

"He came and told me."

"Draco?"

"Jealous, I'm afraid. He's afraid of losing you like he always has in the past. His greatest fear is losing his beloved. Your love is his biggest achievement."

"Does it ever stop?"

"True love never dies, Ivy. It's what you do in this life that affects the next. Always remember that. There is always sacrifice. It's part of it. The good and the bad."

I hear rustling behind me. I turn and find Draco standing in the entrance, looking between me and Seraphina.

"We're ready. The show," he says more to me than to her.

I get up and smile. "I'll see you later."

"Give 'em hell, Ivy. I'll be here if you need me and…" She winks. "Take care of him later."

She means fuck his brains out.

CHAPTER TWENTY-SEVEN
DRACO

I NEVER MEANT to tell her about our daughter, worried the pain of our loss would make her spiral into madness. Madness I've spent years controlling with our love.

After Keir and Lex's act is done, she walks up, and I bow dramatically like I've done so many times before. Perfecting it so I would impress her when she saw me again. Like the first time two people meet and they fall in love. Butterflies.

Trembles deep in your bones when you make love, knowing it's the day you conceive your love child.

"Are you ready for the helicopter?"

"Yes," she mouths.

She is so sexy with her red suede boots covering her thighs.

I lift her off the ground. Her legs open wide in a horizontal split. Her arms stretched wide. I turn her in circles, holding her steady. Her pussy is in my face, and the sweet smell is heaven.

I spin her faster, like we are spinning backward in time. To another place. A place I hope she can remember.

I FEEL ALIVE, the excitement pumping in my veins. The crowd is in awe. I look up and see Nyx flying above, suspended in the air with a seductive smile.

Draco twirls me in the air like a helicopter. The same way we rehearsed, spinning me faster and faster. The crowd fades, then everything around me until I look up and I'm not in the tent. I'm looking straight ahead at a different version of Draco. One without the tattoos. A vintage version.

I look around, and we are seated in the booth at the diner. The same one my mother works except the booths are not shiny but instead have stripes. Red and white like a fifties diner. I look out the window to my right, and all the cars in the parking lot are all sixties classics.

The shiny tabletops catch the light just right. Each booth is separated by slender metal dividers, offering a sense of privacy. The air is filled with the teasing aroma of freshly brewed coffee and sizzling bacon.

Behind the counter is a row of swivel stools. The waitresses, dressed in retro uniforms complete with aprons and paper hats, bustle about with trays balanced expertly on their arms, delivering steaming plates of pancakes and burgers with a smile.

The walls are adorned with vintage memorabilia – old Coca-Cola ads, black-and-white photographs of iconic movie stars, and framed newspaper clippings from the past.

A large chalkboard hangs above the counter, listing the day's specials in colorful chalk writing.

The constant chatter of kids in leather jackets and girls with short hair reminds me of the set of the movie Grease *with John Travolta. The mingling with the clinking of flatware and the occasional burst of laughter.*

"Do you want to go to the lake, Angela?"

I turn in my seat. Angela? I look out the window and catch my reflection in the glass. My face looks similar but different. My hair a different shade. My lips a different shape.

Music starts playing a familiar song. The Angels "My Boyfriend's Back."

"Your favorite song is playing," Draco says.

I look up and he looks like a sixties version of himself. Leather jacket and dark lashes with a dark line under his eyes.

"Angela?"

Oh shit, the lake.

"Yeah," I say with a smile.

He grins. "You don't have to if you're not ready."

"Your brother?"

"He's home. He doesn't start high school until next year, and he's excited. He is dying to go to the same school as Alex."

"Alex?"

"Alexandria." He winks like we are keeping a special secret. "Your best friend."

"Oh, right."

Alex must be Alice. I look around the diner and smile.

It's a flashback.

The song.

The diner.

Draco.

He slides out of the booth and holds out his hand. I look up, and I know in my heart that this moment is special. It means something. I slide my hand in his. My almond-shaped nails are painted a bright pink. My heavy skirt brushes my ankles as he pulls my arm gently so I can stand.

He leans in and brushes his lips against mine. His lips are warm and familiar.

I can hear gasps and giggles in the background.

"He's so hot," one girls says.

"So is she," another girl replies.

"They look so good together," another girl says.

I keep watching him as he drives through the woods in his classic black Impala. "Runaround Sue" by Dion plays from the radio.

He turns on a dirt road. The tires going over rocks. He parks in front of the lake. The moon reflects off the surface. The stars twinkle in the dark sky.

He turns in his seat and caresses my cheek with his thumb. "I love you, Angela. You're my forever."

I lean into his touch. "I love you too," I tell him.

I feel like I've never stopped telling him how much I love him. A ball forms in my throat.

"It's okay to be scared your first time." He says with a smile. "But I think you know that."

"I want to. I'm ready."

He leans in and kisses me softly. Our tongues twirl and taste each other.

He unbuttons my blouse. My breasts set high. He pushes my shoulder-length golden blond hair back and slides off the strap of my vintage bra, but I know in this time it's considered new.

He releases my heavy breasts and caresses my hard pink nipples with his fingers. His head dips and sucks one into his mouth.

I gasp, tilting my head back.

"Draco,"I plead.

In one swift movement, he removes his black leather jacket and undoes the button of his black pants to release his hard cock. He pushes my heavy skirt up my thighs.

Suddenly, I wish I didn't have so many clothes on. So much fabric. I'm sweaty and hot. I'm wet. My clit aches.

He manages to push all the layers of my skirt up my waist and pulls my panties down my thighs.

He looks up. I scoot down, so my back is flat on the seat. The palm of his hand slides up my thigh. He settles between my legs. His cock is hot and heavy against my clit.

"Look at me, Angela,"he demands.

His eyes are dark, and I swear I can see my soul reflected inside his. The Chiffons "Will You Still Love Me Tomorrow"plays like a chant between us.

The tip of his cock glides up and down my clit, working me until I'm writhing under him. He pushes in the tip, and I tense. It's tight, and he's big. I feel full, like I'm going to burst into a thousand pieces.

Sweat drips down his forehead. His arms tremble while he holds his weight so he doesn't crush me. I wrap my arms around him. His face falls between my neck and shoulder, and he pushes the rest of the way, breaking through my barrier.

I gasp. "Draco," I say breathlessly.

It hurts and feels good at the same time. He moves inside me, and I undulate my hips, and he fucks me hard and slow.

"Fuck, you're perfect every time," he rasps against my skin.

I widen my hips and grip his ass, pushing him deeper inside me.

I moan as he moves faster. Our heavy breaths pant between us as we make love under the pure white stars.

We both come together out of breath. The windows are fogged up. His wet black hair is matted against his forehead as he tries to catch his breath.

He's gorgeous.

"I love you, Draco. I'm lost in a timeless dream. In this time and the next. I love the gift of touching and discovering you again and again."

"I love meeting every version of you. No matter what, I love you and I would do anything for you."

My feet touch the ground, and I look up at the red and black tent. The crowd claps and cheers loudly through the air. I'm out of breath from the exhilaration.

Draco watches me intently as I sway my hips in character down the stage. Something passes between us. Recognition.

"You had a vision?" he asks when I sit in the chair in front of the mirror.

I stare at his reflection through the mirror. "How did you know?"

His mouth inches from my ear when he whispers, "It was one of our first times, wasn't it." I meet his eyes, wondering how he knows. "I can see it in your eyes, Ivy. The memory's attached to your soul. Once the circle begins, it is passed on to the soul that will love the next version of us when the time comes."

"Does it ever stop?"I ask.

He straightens. "I don't know. I'm guessing when it is perfect enough."

"What do you mean?"

"When it's the best version of ourselves. The perfect love story. I think but I'm not sure."

"That doesn't exist."

But every girl wants it to exist.

Villain or hero.

Angel or devil.

We all want the perfect love.

"It exists… with us."

CHAPTER TWENTY-EIGHT
DRACO

"I HAVE A SURPRISE FOR YOU," I tell her, handing her an ax.

She's ready. They found one of the girls who was abducted. Dehydrated and starved. Raped and battered. I found the one who took her.

"Show me."

I hand her my phone and wait as she reads the news media article online. She stands with determination in her eyes and the ax in her hand.

Pulling open the door, I watch as her face remains impassive from the smell of death. She walks in, followed by Nyx, Keir, Lex, and the Butcher.

I pull the door closed. "Let the games begin," I announce.

The man hangs from the ceiling by his wrists. Arms spread wide. His ankles are tied together, but he's on his knees, so Ivy can do what she wants.

His beard is matted with blood. His teeth are knocked out and scattered on the floor.

Ivy walks forward, dragging the sharp edge of the ax on the metal floor. It makes a scraping sound as she steps under the light.

She looks magnificent.

"Well, well, well. Look wat wee have here. Another Freak. You're pretty. I bet your pussy smells like that little cunt I fucked until she bled."

"Is that what you did?"Ivy says in a flat tone.

"Oh yeah. I can show you if you'd like." He spits on the ground. "I'll cut you up real nice."

Nyx laughs. "You're in so much trouble, mister," she says in a funny voice. "She's crazier than all of us."

"You should see what happened to the last guy," Lex adds. "That's nothing compared to what she's going to do to you."

Ivy turns and narrows her gaze on the shirt with DTF written across it on the floor.

I lean close. "You didn't think I was actually going to let him move, did you?"

"Come here baby?" The man taunts "I bet you taste nice like them girls."

My gaze flicks to the man. His hair is all sweaty. He's pissed himself about three times already trying to act tough.

His protruding stomach hangs out of his shirt. His pants are sliding off his hip. A ball of pubic hair is stuck to the skin of his lower belly. He's disgusting. A pig. A pedophile. Men like him don't deserve to live.

"You are all a bunch of fucking Freaks. You think you can kill all of us?" He laughs, blood dripping from the corner of his mouth. "You're a pretty whore. I would break you in really good like those little—"

Ivy swings the ax straight into his face, splitting his mouth. His eyes roll upward, looking straight at her and then involuntarily jerk in his skull. Blood doesn't splatter.

Not at first. His legs shake convulsively. His eyes fill with blood. He starts crying, but no sound comes out.

Ivy pulls the ax out, and his face splits awkwardly. You could see the roof of his mouth.

Nyx laughs with glee, clapping her hands together. Ivy swings the ax between his eyes, splitting his skull open. Blood shoots out like a spout bathing her hands. There is a hissing noise from his arteries spraying blood everywhere. The Butcher cuts the ropes. Keir tries to take the ax from Ivy, but she glares and pulls it away from his grasp.

This makes me happy for some reason. She's here. It's her.

The man's body falls on the floor, with one eyelid jerking involuntarily. Brain matter oozes from his open skull. His tongue hangs out like a dog. His arms jerk on the floor.

"Who's the Freak now, huh?" Ivy screams and then laughs at her own outburst. "You're all going to die." She swings the ax hard to the ground, splitting the rest of his skull into pieces. It takes forty-five minutes for him to stop jerking and finally die.

She turns around, covered in blood like she came straight from the set of a horror story. "Did I do good, baby?" she says in a naughty voice. "Do you want to play?'

She's back.

My wife is back.

Her madness is music to my ears.

CHAPTER TWENTY-NINE

THE WARNING BELL rings when I walk in school. I ignore the curious stares at my ripped black tights and short uniform skirt. I'll probably get written up for it.

I walk straight to Alice as she leans on my locker, waiting for me.

"Missed me," I ask coyly.

"Always. How was the show this weekend?"

I tilt my head like I have to think about it. "Bloody fine," I say with a wide smile.

Alice raises a brow. "You're happy they found the missing girl."

"There is more."

"I know." She lowers her voice before Jason and Tommy walk up. "Lazarus told me."

"Well, well. Ivy and the Freak," Jason says slowly.

I laugh. "You mean Alice and the Freak or the Freak and Alice."

"More like the slut and the dyke."

I pout. "I like Freak," I say in a little voice.

"I can be a freak," Jason says, leaning close.

Placing my finger over my black lipstick, I say, "My boyfriend wouldn't like that, Jason."

He finally notices that I'm different. Bolder. I'm dressed different too.

"Who the fuck are you?" Tommy says.

"I'm a Freak. Isn't that what you like to call me or rather—us?"

Jason smiles, and I sense the rapist in him. "I'll show you later."He walks by me and says near my ear, "I'm going to fuck you, Ivy. You're going to like it, and I don't care if you say no."

I giggle, and Alice joins in.

Tommy looks between us like we are crazy. "Dude, what the fuck did you tell her?" He turns away, following Jason. "What the fuck, Jason?" he bellows down the hall over the mob of people rushing to class.

"What are you going to do about them?"Alice asks.

"I'm not sure yet,"I tell her, but I have an idea.

"What did Jason tell you?"

I tell her, and I see the hatred for him in her eyes, but she must see the madness in mine. The one that took over the minute I saw the girl's blurred face and the list of her injuries. It all came back. Memories of the past. Embedded and reincarnated.

"Do you know what we are?"Alice asks.

"Yes."

I do.

"Will it ever stop?"

" I don't know, but the cycle repeats. I just hate the part where it takes time for us to find our way back."

"Do you think we will remember this?"

"I will," I say, caressing her cheek. "I will always find you, Alice. Just like he will."

She smiles. " I love you, and I know."

She knows that when she gives birth to two sons, a soul is created inside us that is reborn upon our death linking us in eternity. I didn't understand it at first, but now I do.

"The house."

"Is the key to it all. It will bring you back, Ivy."

"My son?"I ask, confused.

I had a son. I will have a son. I know about my little girl I can never get back but…

"They didn't tell you."

CHAPTER THIRTY

DRACO

"YOU DIDN'T TELL HER."

"I haven't," I say.

"Why? You confused her."

I look up at Keir. "I didn't."

"Then why didn't you tell her about me?" he says through clenched teeth.

"Because you need to believe it."

"I do believe it. I know it's her. I was there. I saw her come back. The way she looked at you. The way you looked at her. It's hard…"

"What is hard?"

"To know that my parents died and they came back to fall in love when I was supposed to die with them the last time."

"She saved you."

"I didn't want to be saved. I want my mother and father."

"She did it because she loved you, Keir. She didn't want children at first because it would slow her down in trying to save the others, but she loved you, and this time, she is going to need you. You have a gift. A chance to find love."

"Are you listening to yourself? You're my father reincarnated into someone else and so is my mother."

"So will you, Keir. The house doesn't bring babies unless you're a Hades. I'm sorry for hitting you the other day. I was afraid…"

"That I would mistake her for the girl of my dreams when she's my mother?"

"Yeah."

"I knew it was her," he says, grabbing his knives. "I felt it inside."

I set the jars on the floor. Keir turns on the light. I hear muffled cries from the two assholes tied to the electric chairs I found in the basement at the house. They still do their job.

I adjust my top hat and push my coat out of the way as Keir plays with their heads.

"You didn't think I'd let you call her a slut, did you?" Keir says, making the knives appear and disappear.

I stand and watch the horror in their eyes when they recognize me.

Keir starts cutting them open.

I smile. "You did say you wanted to see the show." Then, they scream in agony. "Now, who's the slut and the Freak?"

CHAPTER THIRTY-ONE

Mrs. Hades,

When our eyes first met, I fell in love. It was a bond so profound, so enduring, it seemed to have weathered countless lifetimes. The sort of connection that clings to your soul, refusing to let go. The sort of love worth fighting for, worth sacrificing for, worth dying for. I understood then that this love was relentless. Even death itself couldn't extinguish it. It was compelled to release its hold on us. And what remains now are the most exquisite memories etched into the fabric of time.

In every lifetime, our souls instinctively search for one another, irresistibly pulled by an unbreakable connection that transcends the constraints of time and space.

Our love remains forever, intricately woven into the very essence of being, fated to reunite again. We will find each other…forever.

True Love Never Dies

Eternally,

Mr. D Hades.

"THAT IS BEAUTIFUL. Who was Mrs. Hades?" I ask curiously.

Draco looks up, and I can't get over how gorgeous he is, but he's emotionally unavailable. He's the hottest guy in school. I don't know why he would let me read something so personal belonging to his family. I don't know why he watches me in class.

"Her name was Ivy Hades."

The End

Want more of this world? Want more of Ivy, Alice, Draco and Lazarus?
Lovers Fate
True Love Never Dies
Coming 10-24-24
Scan the QR code for upcoming releases and links to preorder

ABOUT THE AUTHOR

From the mind of Carmen Rosales, born with a love for macabre and a penchant for romance, Delilah Croww found her calling in Gothic horror. She transports readers to hauntingly beautiful realms where love and fear collide and where heroes and heroines must battle not only for their hearts but also for their very lives. Her writing is as enchanting as it is eerie, and her stories will linger with you long after you've turned the final page. Scan below for more.